HER AMISH FARM

AMISH BONNET SISTERS BOOK 18

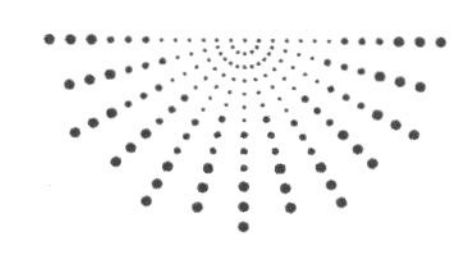

SAMANTHA PRICE

This book is a work of fiction. Any resemblance to any person, living or dead, is purely coincidental. The personal names have been invented by the author, and any likeness to the name of any person, living or dead, is purely coincidental.

CHAPTER ONE

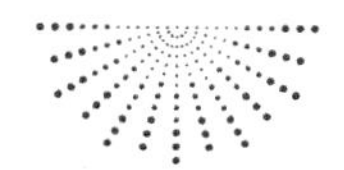

In her bare feet, Cherish Baker sprinted across the cold floorboards when a knock sounded on the front door. When she opened it, she was surprised to see Florence. She and the girls had just finished their Saturday chores in the orchard. Had someone done something wrong? Cherish fixed a smile on her face. "Hi, Florence." She stepped back to allow her through. "Come in. Everyone's in the kitchen. Ada's here too."

"I thought that was her buggy." Florence looked at Levi, who was asleep in his chair with a newspaper on his chest. "Everyone's in the kitchen except for Levi, it seems."

"Yes," Cherish whispered.

Florence followed Cherish through to the kitchen.

Ada was the first to speak to Florence. "Don't you know if you want to use the front or the back door?"

"What do you mean?" Florence asked.

"Most people either come in the front door or the back door every time they come to someone's house. You're unpredictable." Ada looked at the others. "Florence can't make up her mind which one she prefers. It's never one or the other."

"I'm not sure why I do that. Today, I found myself at the front of the house."

Ada laughed. "Your legs must be disconnected from your brain. Or they have a mind of their own."

Florence moved closer to the table. "How are you anyway, Ada?"

"Ah, can't complain."

Cherish wanted to say that wasn't true because she was always complaining, but then Ada might cancel the upcoming trip to the farm.

"What are you doing back here, Florence? Haven't you had enough of us for one day?" Favor asked, jokingly.

"Work's finished for the day, isn't it?" Wilma blinked rapidly. "Surely you're not making the girls work extra on a Saturday afternoon?"

"No, not at all. I have recent news, and also I have old news that I realized I haven't told you."

"Have a seat with us," *Mamm* said.

"Oh, I can't wait. I love to hear news." Favor clapped her hands while *Mamm* scowled at her and covered her ears against the noise.

Cherish sat down next to Florence. "What's the news?"

Florence looked around. "Where is everybody?"

Mamm sighed. "As you would expect, Hope wasted no time going off to be with Fairfax. Adam picked up Bliss, and I have no idea where they went."

Favor said, "He usually takes her back to his workshop

to show her what he and Andrew Weeks have been working on."

Ada nodded. "And don't you two get any ideas. You don't have to find men like your sisters did, so young. Wait until you're at least twenty. Twenty-two is better."

Cherish wasn't happy with Ada. "You were the one who matched Mercy."

"I was asked to find her someone suitable."

"Jah, she wanted to marry young," *Mamm* said. "Ada knew the perfect man, her own nephew."

Cherish didn't want to hear that story again. "So, Miriam is too old to marry, and Mercy was too young?"

"Exactly." Ada picked up her tea and sipped it. "Ah, nice and hot, just how I like it. Now, what is your news, Florence?"

"My news is that we'll be digging the foundations for the new house. It's all starting on Monday."

Ada's eyebrows flew upward. "You'll be doing that yourselves?"

"Not me personally, or Carter. I meant the workers will do it, the builders."

Ada laughed. "I knew Carter wouldn't be doing anything with his hands."

"No, he uses his brain," *Mamm* said.

When Ada scowled to show she wasn't happy about what *Mamm* said, Cherish did her best to divert their attention by being extra loud. "I'm so excited that your new house is beginning after all this time. You've been planning it for a year, haven't you?"

"More than that. Ever since we married, and I moved

in, but it's probably been a year since we got the architect involved."

"Yes, the cottage is rather small," said *Mamm*. "That is exciting, and what is your other news?"

"Wait," Ada said. "Is your new house going up next to the cottage?"

"Between the cottage and the road."

Ada turned to Wilma. "It's a shame you don't have that land now. It turns out the land could've been worth a sum."

"I know, but at the time, we had to do something. We had many bad seasons due to crazy weather. We had to sell that section of land to help save the orchard, and it did."

Ada turned to Florence. "Continue."

"Well, it's not my news. I found out today that Earl and Miriam are getting married."

"We already know that," Cherish said. "They're getting married at the end of the year, just like Fairfax and Hope."

Florence laughed. "No, I forgot to say they're getting married in a few weeks and not at the end of the year. They brought the wedding forward."

Mamm put her cup down heavily onto the saucer. "What?"

"Why didn't they tell us?" Ada turned to Wilma. "Did you know this, Wilma?"

"I didn't."

Favor put her hand on *Mamm's* shoulder. "*Mamm,* he didn't leave on the best of terms. Maybe he doesn't want you at the wedding, and that's why he didn't tell you himself."

Cherish recalled the dreadful scene of a few weeks ago when Miriam and Earl left in a rush. It was all Ada's fault because she'd tried to match Miriam up with Ezekiel Troyer, the pig farmer. Then there were *Mamm* and Ada's awful comments about their age difference. Earl was outraged when he found out, and he and Miriam left immediately and went back home to Ohio.

Wilma pursed her lips. "Nonsense. I'll still go. I'm sure he won't mind if we're at the wedding. What do you think, Ada?"

"I suppose if they insist on going ahead with getting married despite our giving them our best advice, we should go to the wedding. Up until the last minute, he can change his mind."

Cherish noticed Florence's face twitched with concern. Earl must've said he didn't want them there. "We're going to the farm in a few days. I hope we'll be back in time for the wedding."

"We can only stay for five days at the farm, Cherish."

"Thank you, Ada. Five days are better than no days."

Florence smiled at Cherish. "You must be excited to be going back there, Cherish."

"I would go too, but I'm staying here to work," Favor said.

Cherish glared at Favor for that comment. Was her sister trying to make her look bad for checking on the farm? Did Favor want someone to praise her for staying? "I am super excited to see how it's coming along. I think Malachi is doing a good job, but I still need to keep my eye on the place. I don't want it to get run down or anything of the kind."

"I think you should be delighted with him," *Mamm* said. "I think he's running the place well, and don't forget he's the only one who put his hand up for the job, so be nice to him."

"I thought you were worried about what he was doing with the farm, Cherish," said Favor.

Before Cherish could say anything, *Mamm* said, "Bishop Zachariah wouldn't have recommended him if he didn't know he was going to do a good job."

Ada said, "But he's the bishop's nephew, Wilma."

"But still, he wouldn't."

Ada pursed her lips. "I suppose that's true enough. Any more news?" Ada asked Florence.

"No more news. That's all I have."

"Well, I have some news, too," said Wilma. "Ada and Samuel have agreed to go with me to visit Honor and Mercy. I'll be there for the births just like I was there for their first babies."

"That is good news. I hope they can come here soon after that. We haven't seen them in forever. They've only been back here once since they left," Favor said.

"I hope they visit too. Then Iris can meet her cousins." Florence stood. "I must get home. I just thought you'd like to know Earl's news as soon as possible."

Favor jumped to her feet. "Before you go, Florence. I'll quickly show you what I've done with the vegetable garden."

"I'd love to see it."

Once Favor and Florence left, Ada and Wilma stared at one another. Cherish knew they had a lot to say.

Ada stared at her empty cup. "I'd like another, please, and thank you, Cherish."

"Sure." Cherish took her cup to the sink and then filled up the teakettle.

"Well, Wilma, what do you think of Earl bringing his wedding date forward by a whole six months?" Ada asked.

"I'm not happy about it. I tried to talk sense into him and her, but what can you do with people who won't listen?"

"That's exactly right. You can't do anything." Ada blew out a deep breath.

Cherish lit the gas stove and then placed the teakettle over the flame.

Ada raised herself off her chair to see what Cherish was doing. "I hope you haven't filled it too much. It'll take forever to boil, and I don't like waiting."

"I only half-filled it."

"Ah, *gut*."

When Ada sat back down, Wilma said, "I won't say I'm not upset about it because I am."

"He should listen to you, Wilma. My opinion shouldn't matter to him, but yours should. You're the closest thing to a mother he has."

Wilma stared into her half-gone cup of tea. "It seems it doesn't mean much to him. It never has. We never got along, not really."

"You did. Don't say you didn't, Wilma, because that's not accurate."

"If we did, it was so long ago that I don't remember."

"As a child, he would've seen you as the loving mother that you were. You were so good to those children. You treated them as your own."

Cherish leaned against the countertop. Then she saw Ada lifting the teapot, so she rushed over to take it from her. Then Cherish set about emptying the old leaves and placing new ones in the pot. "More tea for you too, *Mamm?*"

"Of course." *Mamm* sighed then and said to Ada, "I don't know what I did to make him turn against me."

"And he didn't call you about the new arrangements and tell you himself. Or he could've written you a letter."

"The letter might be on its way." Cherish put the lid back on the tea caddy.

Ada stared at Cherish. "Did anyone ask you anything?"

"No, but I'm here, and I didn't know I had to ask if I could speak."

"That's what hurt," said Wilma. "We find out through Florence like she is the real one who matters in his life, and not us."

"What does Levi think about it? That's what I'd like to know." Ada gave a nod.

Wilma breathed out heavily. "Levi never comments about anything. And I don't like to say anything because he thinks I'm complaining all the time when I'm not. I'm just having a conversation and telling him how I feel."

"No, you're not complaining. I agree with you there. We did everything we could." Ada patted Wilma's hand.

Cherish decided it was time to join in again. "Did what you could about what?"

Mamm pressed her lips together. "I told you not to eavesdrop, but it just goes in one ear and out the other."

"I'm in the same room, just feet away from you. That's not eavesdropping."

Mamm continued, "You'll hear something bad about yourself one day when you're listening in to others, and that will teach you."

"Yes, that will serve you right," said Ada.

"Too late for that because I've already heard lots of horrible things about myself."

Ada shook her head. "I don't doubt it for a moment."

When the kettle boiled, Cherish filled the teapot and placed it back on the table along with Ada's empty cup. "Excuse me then. I guess you won't mind pouring your own if that will mean I can leave you both to talk on your own without fear of me listening." Cherish headed into the living room without waiting for an answer.

"Your rudeness will catch up with you one day, my girl," Ada called out to her.

Cherish did not comment. She found Levi sitting in his usual chair, awake now, and reading his newspaper. This was the perfect time to ask him something. "Levi, can I talk to you for a moment?"

Levi looked up over the top of his paper. He lowered it, revealing his long graying beard. "Yes, what is it?"

Cherish sat down on the opposite couch, trying to calm herself the best she could. Levi had been reasonable lately, and there was a chance he might say yes to what she was about to ask. It didn't stop her from being nervous, though. "It's about my one day a week at the café. I'm going to the farm and I won't be there."

"*Jah,* I know this. They'll have to find someone else to work in your stead."

"That's right; they will. And I thought it might be a good idea, and a nice thing, if Bliss could take over my one day when I'm gone. It would mean a lot to her, and it would just be one single day." She made sure she kept emphasizing the word 'one.'

Levi folded the paper over and set it down on the table in front of him. Then he moved his mouth sideways, causing his whole beard to move to one side along with it. "Have you two cooked this up among yourselves?"

"Oh, no. I haven't mentioned a word to her because if you say no, she'll be so disappointed. You know how she loves working at the café. It'll be like a special treat for her if you allow her to do it."

He rubbed his beard. "One day, you say? To take your place, is that right?"

"Yes, she's been working so hard in the orchard, and it would be like a small reward. It would make her happy."

"I don't see that will be a problem." He picked up the paper again.

Cherish could scarcely believe her ears. "You mean, she can?"

"Yes, if it's all right with the people you work for."

"Yes, it is. I already asked Rocky, the boss, and he said that would be fine because she knows the routines from before when she worked there. He'd rather Bliss be there than someone new who was just filling in for a day. Rocky started that new second café, and he's had to employ a lot of new people, and..."

"I get the picture. I already said yes, Cherish."

"You mean it?"

"I do. Now you can tell Bliss. Unless she knows about it already. Does she?"

Why didn't anyone trust her? "No, she doesn't. I said that, and I meant it. The only thing is, what about Florence? Will she mind Bliss having a day off? I'll be gone too."

"I'll work instead of her for that day."

"Thanks, Levi. Florence won't mind then if you're prepared to do that." She jumped up and hugged him.

"Whoa. It's only for one day, isn't it?" He eyed her suspiciously.

"One single solitary day. Yes, that's right. You don't know how happy this will make her."

Levi chuckled. Cherish bounded up to her room to keep packing for the farm. There she'd stay until Bliss came home, and then she'd tell her about working at the café in her place.

CHAPTER TWO

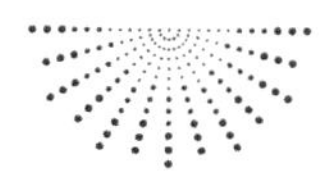

After Florence admired Favor's efforts in the vegetable garden, she walked home through the orchard. She was continually thankful that the orchard had come back to her. It didn't matter that she had to share it with her family members.

The orchard had stayed in the family, and that's what her father would've wanted. To her, the orchard was not an object or a piece of real estate; it was a living and breathing thing, brought to life by her father's vision and hard work. Now she could teach others the skills her father had taught her, and that way the orchard would continue to the next generation.

It wouldn't have been possible if God hadn't softened Levi's heart. He had been taking the orchard in a wrong direction, and he'd also been thinking of selling. The notion of selling had suddenly stopped, as though God had whispered in Levi's ear.

Moving closer to home, Florence wandered down the

rows of trees, admiring the buds and the green leaves that were sprouting. Spring was nearly upon them, Florence's favorite time of year. Soon the orchard would be full of blossoms, bringing with them hope and new life.

Now that her half-sisters had gotten into a routine with their orchard work, Florence wondered if her life could get any better.

Years back, her life was full of toil and hardship, being like a mother to the younger six Baker girls, being in charge of the household and the orchard. So much had been on her shoulders. Now she had Carter, her new orchard on their property, and they'd been able to buy the orchard on the other side of the Baker Orchard. They were also able to employ people to manage it.

When her cottage came into view, she saw Carter on the porch. Spot caught sight of her and bounded toward her. She always got such a welcome from their dog unless he was fast asleep on the couch.

She slipped through the wire fence, and then Spot reached her. "Hello, boy." She looked up at Carter as he walked down to meet her.

"Is Iris asleep?" she asked.

"Fast asleep."

"I hope she sleeps tonight."

"I'm sure she'll be awake in a minute. If not, I'll wake her. We don't want her waking at four in the morning again. How did they take the news about Earl and Miriam?" Carter put his arm around her shoulders, and they walked back to the house.

"It's hard to tell. They were shocked and said Earl

didn't take their advice. Wilma and Ada said a few more things when I was outside looking at Favor's vegetable patch. They didn't know I heard them."

"I can only imagine."

"They were deciding whether they'll go to the wedding or not."

"What if they're not invited? It would be awkward having them there after what they did to Miriam."

"Our Amish weddings aren't like that. People hear about it, and they go. No one's officially invited at all, at least not in any of the communities I know about."

"I didn't know. Are we going?"

"Of course we are."

Carter chuckled. "I thought so."

"I wouldn't miss it. Besides, they need some family support."

WHEN CHERISH SAW Bliss come home with Adam a couple of hours later, she ran down the stairs to talk with her while Adam tended to the horse.

She stood on the porch, watching them while they got out of the buggy. Bliss was different when Adam was around. Her face lit up and even though she was usually happy, she was even more so around him.

Bliss looked up and saw her watching. She said something to Adam and then hurried over. "What's happening, Cherish?"

"I have some great news for you." Cherish fell into one

of the porch chairs and propped her feet against the porch railing.

Bliss sat on the other chair. "How good is this news? Let me guess. *Mamm* is letting you have another budgie, only it'll be mine to look after, or is she allowing me to have another rabbit?"

"I said great news. I didn't say a blinding miracle."

The two girls put their heads together and laughed.

"Well, it's not quite as exciting as that, but I have cleared it with everybody for you to take over from me when I go to the farm."

"Take over your chores? How's that good news for me?" Bliss frowned, then her gaze wandered to Adam, and the frown left.

Bliss couldn't take her eyes from Adam. She was always admiring him. Or maybe she was making sure he didn't run away.

Cherish looked at Adam, too. He sure looked good today— all tall and muscled with his white shirt billowing in the breeze, and his dark golden hair dancing around his chiseled face. It was a shame Bliss had stolen him away from her. "*Nee,* not chores. Take over my shift at the café."

Bliss's attention left Adam immediately. "No way! Really? I'm allowed to work at the café while you're at the farm?"

Cherish managed to pull her gaze away from Adam. "Yes, and of course, you can keep the money for that day and any tips you get as well. I'll only be gone a week, so that'll only be the one shift. Unless I'm too tired when I come back, and you have to do another day for me."

Bliss smiled so much her cheeks got extra chubby. "Did *Dat* truly say yes?"

Cherish nodded. "He did."

Bliss lunged forward and wrapped her arms around her. Cherish was getting squashed into the chair and had to put her arms up to remove Bliss.

"Thank you so much, Cherish. I don't know how you did it. You got permission from Rocky, *Dat,* and Florence?"

Cherish licked her lips. "Nearly all those people."

Bliss's shoulders drooped. "I knew it was too good to be true. You haven't cleared it with *Dat,* and he'll say no. But, you just said he allowed me, so I don't get it."

"No! You've got it all wrong. If you listen instead of talking over the top of me, you'll understand what I'm trying to say. He said yes, but we just haven't asked Florence, but I'm sure she'll say yes because your *vadder* said he would take your place that day."

"He said that?"

"Jah."

"Thank you so much for doing this, Cherish. I'll look forward to it. What's Marlie like? I've heard all the things you say about her."

"She's not as easy to get along with as Rocky, but don't worry, you'll be fine. She'll watch you all the time, but as long as you're doing everything correctly, it won't matter."

"I hope so."

"Rocky's got the new café across town, and he's having trouble finding good staff, and he knows what a good worker you are. He was happy I suggested you."

"Thank you, Cherish. You're the best sister ever."

Cherish laughed. "I know."

When they saw Adam walk toward them, that was the end of their conversation. No one could get any sense out of Bliss when that man was around.

CHAPTER THREE

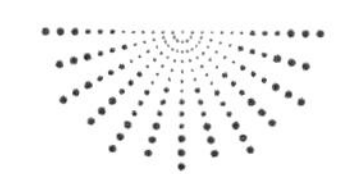

The next day was the first Sunday in the month, and there was no meeting that day, but it was still their day of rest. Levi took the opportunity of having everyone home to gather the girls and Wilma for a family meeting.

"Girls, there is something exciting to tell you." Everyone looked at Levi and waited for him to continue. "As you know, Krystal has gone and she helped out around the place. She was a hard worker. Wilma and I decided we need an extra pair of hands around the place."

"Yes, we need more help." Wilma gave a nod.

"That's why Cousin Debbie is coming to stay with us for a while until I'm feeling better, and I'll be able to help out a bit more around the place."

Cherish looked at Bliss, who didn't look happy with the news. "Do you know her very well, Bliss?"

"Jah, I do. It's *Dat's* brother's daughter. Are you sure this is the right thing, *Dat?* If we all pitched in a little more..."

"That's right."

"Why didn't you talk to me about it?" Bliss asked her father.

"Wilma needs help, and we can use an extra helper around the orchard."

"I do need assistance," Wilma said

"Don't you like her?" Cherish asked Bliss.

"Of course I do. She's my cousin. I'm shocked, that's all."

"How did you get her to come here?" Cherish asked Levi.

"The thing is, and this is a sore point to talk about, her mother is moving out of the family home to stay with her sister."

"That means Debbie's parents are divorcing?" Cherish asked.

"They're separating is what that means, I think," Hope told Cherish.

"Oh."

"Let's not think about that part of it. Let's say that Debbie's parents both think it best that she live elsewhere for a while until all the adjustments are made." Levi stroked his beard.

Now it was clear that Debbie's parents were trying to get rid of her. It wasn't about them needing help. Levi was trying to sell it to them rather than saying they'd gain another unwanted visitor. They'd only just got rid of Krystal.

"She's a pleasant girl, and you'll all get along with her fine."

"How long is she staying?" asked Favor.

"As long as need be," Wilma said.

Favor sighed. "The poor girl, she has nowhere to stay because her mother and father are getting divorced. It makes me want to cry."

"They're not getting divorced," Levi told her.

"Don't you listen, Favor? They already said her parents aren't divorcing," Hope commented, glaring at her younger sister.

Favor shook her head. "Whatever they're doing, it doesn't sound good if they don't want Debbie to stay there. I didn't mean to say divorce. I meant separating."

"Well, why didn't you say it?" Hope asked. "You make everything sound terrible all the time."

Cherish said, "Now, girls, stop squabbling. I'm happy for a new face around here. I'm getting quite bored with the old ones."

Everyone laughed at her. "You're a fine one to tell people to stop squabbling, Cherish." *Mamm* put her hand over her mouth and giggled.

"Your *mudder* also thought it would be good to have Debbie here for when she visits Honor and Mercy, too."

"Are you going to see them too, *Dat?*" Bliss asked.

"*Nee*. I'll stay here."

"Can I go up with you, *Mamm?*" Cherish asked. "I'll help out. I've never seen their first babies."

"Neither have any of us," said Hope. "If anyone should go it would be me."

"*Nee*. Ada and Samuel are coming up with me, and that's all. Debbie will be here to take over my home duties while you're all at the orchard."

Hope said, "That's nice. Debbie needs somewhere to stay and we need the help of an extra person."

"How old is Debbie?" Favor asked.

"She's a couple of years older than Bliss."

Cherish gulped. *Great! Someone else to boss me about.*

"We can all enjoy today, our day of rest. What are we all doing?" *Mamm* asked.

Bliss sat tall in her seat. "I've got something to do. Adam is coming to take me out."

Levi rubbed his beard. "Where to?"

"I'm not sure yet. We'll probably drive around like we always do and grab a bite to eat somewhere."

Wilma turned up her nose. "Sounds very casual. Why don't you pack a picnic basket? It's perfect weather for it."

"Maybe next time."

"What about you, Hope?" *Mamm* asked.

"Fairfax has painted the cottage, and he wants me to see it."

Levi's eyebrows rose. "His cottage where he's living?"

"Yes, he's living back on his parents' old property. He's been there for some time."

"Well, you can walk there."

"That's what I was going to do. He's sleeping in this morning. It's the only day he gets a chance to do that."

"I wish I was allowed to sleep in," said Cherish.

Wilma glared at her. "No good sleeping through your life. What will you do today, Cherish?"

"I haven't thought about it yet." Cherish shrugged her shoulders.

"You can help me consider which bedroom we'll give Debbie."

Favor pouted. "No one has bothered to ask me what I'm doing today."

"They haven't asked me either. All right, what will you do today, Favor?" *Mamm* asked.

"Sit around and be bored, I guess. I have nothing to do."

Mamm smiled, totally unaware of Favor's feelings. "Levi and I are going visiting after lunch."

Cherish laughed. "Let me guess, Ada and Samuel's?"

"We might go there," said Levi.

When there was a loud knock on the front door, Wilma rose from her chair. "Who would that be at this hour on a Sunday morning?"

Cherish jumped up. "You stay, *Mamm,* I'll go see." She hurried to open the door. Standing in front of her was Eddie, the beekeeper. "Eddie!" With so much going on, she'd forgotten about him and his crush he had on her. The awful memories flooded back.

"Hiya, Cherish."

"How have you been?" Cherish searched her memory banks, figuring out how they'd left things. The last time she saw him was when she'd brought Miriam to his house to learn about beekeeping. He then said he didn't want a dishonest girl like Krystal and that he preferred her. She was sure she didn't say anything to cause him to believe his feelings were returned, so... what was he doing here?

He stepped closer, and she backed away a little. "I've missed you."

"Oh." She hoped none of her family overheard. "Have you heard from Krystal?"

"She keeps calling, but I keep not answering."

"Oh."

"You seem funny today. Everything okay, Cherish?"

She sucked in a quick breath of air. "I'm surprised you're here, that's all."

"Can I come in?"

She stared at him, wondering what to say. Her family was inside, and it would be embarrassing for them to know Eddie liked her. She moved onto the porch and closed the door behind her. "Why don't we go for a walk instead? It's a lovely day for it."

"Sure, if that's what you want."

She walked past him and jumped down the porch steps. With him beside her, she rushed toward the covering of the trees. Once they were nearly at the first row, she knew she had to be honest with him. It was the only way. "I like you, Eddie—"

"Cool."

"Let me finish. I really like you as a friend, but it can never be anything more." She searched his face. He didn't seem upset at all.

"You might be like that now, but I'm prepared to wait."

This wasn't good. So much for the truth. "Wait for what?"

"For you to change your mind."

She didn't know what else to say.

He continued, "Your sister, Florence, left your community to marry outside of your group so that means there's a door that might come open for me."

"That's true. She married Carter, and she left us. When I'm older, I won't even be here. I'm moving to my farm."

"There are always ways to work around things. I've

never met a girl like you, and I'm not going to give up. I'll wait for you for as long as I have to."

"Cherish!"

They both stopped when they heard someone calling Cherish's name.

"That's my mother. I'll have to go, Eddie." She stared at him, waiting for him to say he'd go, but he didn't.

All she could do was start walking back. He followed.

When they were nearly at the house, *Mamm* was staring at them from the porch. "Is that you, Eddie?" *Mamm* called out.

"It is, Mrs. Baker."

"Bruner," Cherish whispered.

"Sorry. I mean, Mrs. Bruner."

"I didn't know where you'd gotten to, Cherish. We still haven't finished our family meeting."

"Yikes," he whispered to Cherish. "What's all that about?"

"Nothing much." She looked up at her mother. "I'm coming." Then she said to Eddie, "I'm sorry, but we *were* in the middle of something."

"That's okay. You could've told me. Come visit me sometime, okay?"

"Sure."

"When?" He fixed his gaze upon her.

"Um, soon."

"You mean it?"

"Yes." Cherish headed to her mother while Eddie went back to his car.

Mamm folded her arms. "What did he want so early in the day, and on a Sunday of all days?"

"Nothing much."

"Did he bring us some honey?"

"*Nee, Mamm.* We have boxes of their honey."

"I know that. I was only asking."

They both stood on the porch and watched Eddie drive away.

"You didn't answer me."

Cherish looked into her mother's pale brown eyes. "What?"

"Why was Eddie here?"

"I told you, nothing much."

"Didn't look like 'nothing much' to me, and why were you two sneaking off into the orchard?"

Cherish shrugged her shoulders. "No reason. I wasn't sneaking."

Mamm's mouth pinched, and she leaned down and shook her finger in Cherish's face. "You used to sneak off at night to see boys. Now you're doing it in the middle of the day."

"It's not like that. It wasn't like that back then either."

"No, it never is with you. I forbid you to see Eddie again."

Cherish couldn't keep the smile from her face. This was perfect. "Okay. I can agree to that."

"And, we could always do with more honey." *Mamm* turned around. "Now, let's finish our family meeting."

Cherish followed her mother. She couldn't wait to call Eddie and say her mother had forbidden her to see him. So it wouldn't hurt his feelings, she decided to tell him she was grounded for an unforeseeable time. It sounded so much better.

CHAPTER FOUR

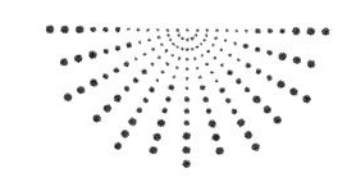

Cherish needed to call Daniel Whitcombe. She looked for his number in the family notebook in the barn. It didn't say Daniel Whitcombe. It was Daniel Withers. Why had she been calling him Daniel Whitcombe these past months?

Before she got to the bottom of that mystery, she called Eddie. He didn't pick up the phone, and it went to his voicemail. She left the message telling him she was grounded, and she'd call him when she was ungrounded. After that, she dialed the number of the newspaper.

"Good morning. I'd like to speak to Daniel Withers, please."

"One moment."

"Hello," he said a minute later.

"Why have I been calling you Daniel Whitcombe all this time when your name is Daniel Withers?"

"Oh, is this Cherish?"

"You know it is."

"My name was Withers, and I changed it to Whitcombe a short time ago."

"Why would you do that? Are you hiding from someone? In witness protection?"

He laughed. "I wouldn't be a reporter if I was in witness protection. No. I thought Whitcombe sounded more of a substantial name for a reporter or an anchorman, which is what I hope to be one day. Withers was wishy-washy."

"It sounded fine. Where did you get Whitcombe from?"

"It was my mother's maiden name."

"You might have told me. I asked to speak to Daniel Withers, and they put me through. Maybe you should tell the receptionist that's not your real name now."

"They don't care. They know me as both those names. Although for the paper—news articles—it's definitely Whitcombe."

"Oh. That is confusing."

"Anyway, now we've got that out of the way, what can I do for you, Cherish Baker?"

"I'm calling to let you know that I'm still working on getting you that other story, okay?"

"Let me correct you there. Two other stories. Unless the one story you bring me is sensational—out of this world scandalous."

Now it seemed even further out of reach. "And who's going to be the judge of that?"

"Me, of course. Don't worry. I'll be honest."

"You're not the most ethical person I've ever come across."

"Don't be like that, Cherish. I'm trying to get ahead in life."

She wasn't going to have that conversation with him again. He was getting ahead by stepping on other people, but it was no use reasoning with him. "Please don't do anything until you hear from me again, okay? I'm going to my farm, and I'll be gone for about a week."

"I won't."

"Will you give me your word on that?" Cherish asked.

"I will. I'm not nearly finished writing the stories anyway. They've got to be brilliant. I'll only get one shot at this."

"Thank you, Daniel W... whatever your last name is."

"It's Whitcombe. And I must've told you that, otherwise how would you have known the name?"

"Hmm, that's true. It's probably on that business card you gave me."

"Or, I could've changed it to Whitcombe by the time I wrote that story about your father and the orchard."

"Stepfather. And don't remind me of that dreadful story."

"Everyone liked it."

"Not anyone I know. Goodbye, Daniel."

"Goodbye, Cherish."

When she hung up the phone's receiver, she turned around to see Favor.

"Who were you talking to?" Favor asked, her head tilted to one side.

"Daniel, the reporter."

"Why?"

"It's not hard to guess, is it? I just want to be sure that he doesn't write what he said he was going to."

"He probably will, and there's nothing you can do about it."

"I've got to do all I can."

"If you say so. Have you talked to *Mamm* about it yet?"

Cherish headed out of the barn. "No, I could never talk about anything like that with her. She'd be so upset."

Favor followed her. "You don't know that for sure. You don't know how someone's going to be until you tell them."

"One thing I know, it'll be another thing that's all my fault."

"I heard from Krystal yesterday afternoon."

Cherish couldn't believe she was only hearing about this now. She stopped walking. "What did she say?"

"She said she's re-evaluating her life, and she's going to make some big changes."

"That sounds good. Sounds like something she needs to do."

"And then she said she's not going to talk to me for a while because she wants to have a clear head when she makes her decisions."

Cherish didn't know if that was good or bad. She'd have to believe it was good.

"Hey, let's find out more about Debbie."

Favor smiled. "Okay. How are we going to do that?"

"Ask Bliss, of course. And we better hurry before Adam gets here."

"Or before he takes her away somewhere with him."

"Exactly."

CHAPTER FIVE

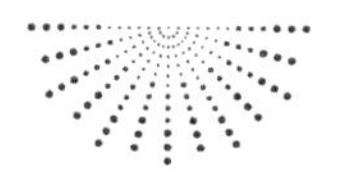

Favor and Cherish found Bliss in her bedroom, changing.

"Why are you getting out of your dress?" asked Favor. "It's a perfectly fine dress, and it's not dirty or anything."

Bliss smoothed the dress down with her hands. "This is a nicer one."

Cherish joined in. "It's perfectly fine, but so was the other one."

"Did you two come here to pick on me?"

"No. At least I didn't." Cherish sat down on the bed.

Favor said, "We came here to find out about Debbie."

Bliss put on her apron, tying the strings at the back. "You'll find out for yourselves soon enough."

Favor sat down with Cherish, who groaned and lay down on the bed and looked up at the ceiling. "I want to know how long she'll be here. It was hard getting used to Krystal being here. Do we need another stranger?"

"She's not exactly a stranger. She's Bliss's cousin," Favor said.

Cherish half sat up, resting on her elbows. "At least we know Debbie is a real person, not like Krystal."

"All I can say is what I already said. You'll find out for yourselves soon enough."

"It's not telling us anything. What do you think about her?" asked Cherish.

"She's a perfectly delightful human being."

"Good. Then why the hesitation when Levi mentioned her? You don't seem excited she's coming."

"Nothing much excites me these days. I take everything in my stride. It's something you both will know when you're my age."

Favor looked over her shoulder at Cherish and then said to Bliss, "You're talking as though you're much older than us, and you're not much older at all."

"No, you're not," added Cherish. "What does she look like?"

Bliss gave a casual shrug of her shoulders. "She's okay."

Now Cherish was more concerned. Bliss was acting weird. "What does that mean?"

"Oh, you want details?"

Favor laughed. "Of course we want details. We want to know everything about her."

"She has green eyes and black hair, and her face is oval-shaped. She gets along with everybody. You two will like her."

Cherish sat up. "Will we, though? You seem doubtful about her coming here. You're not excited, and you get carried away by the smallest little thing."

"I do like her. There's nothing wrong with her. I'm just not excited. Do I have to be excited about everything?"

"Strange her parents separating like they have," said Favor. "I've only heard of two couples separating, and they were old. Older than Debbie's parents would be."

"Maybe they are really old—are they Bliss?"

"They're not very old, same age as *Dat,* or thereabouts. "

"He's old," said Favor.

Bliss then removed her prayer *kapp* and pulled a brush through her hair.

Favor jumped to her feet. "Can I do that for you?"

"Sure."

Favor took the brush and ran it through Bliss's hair, which went down past her waist.

"Can I braid it as well?"

"You sure can. It'll save me doing it."

While they were doing that, Cherish lay back down and put her head on Bliss's pillows. Something told her there was more to this Debbie person. But no matter what she was like, anything would be an improvement on Krystal.

"She's arriving a few days after you come back from the farm, Cherish."

That put a smile on Cherish's face. "I can hardly believe I'm going back there. It's been so long."

"You're so lucky, Cherish. You get to go somewhere. *Mamm* gets to go to Connecticut in a few months, and I'm always stuck here." Favor pouted. "I'm not even allowed to visit Krystal."

Cherish's nose twitched. "I don't know why you'd want to."

"I want to go somewhere. And, Krystal is still my friend. She always will be. We spent all day and night together for months. We became so close."

Favor was kidding herself. For most of that time, she was under the delusion that her friend was Caroline, rather than an imposter who'd 'borrowed' the name.

"Are you finished with my hair now?" Bliss asked. "He'll be here soon."

"Yeah, hold still."

Cherish got out of bed. "I'll watch for him." She sat on the windowsill staring down the driveway and further onto the road. There was no use trying to get information out of Bliss about Debbie, but one person was aware of everything that was going on.

That was Ada.

Cherish might have to wait until they were driving to the farm to find out more. The long car trip would surely loosen Ada's tongue.

CHAPTER SIX

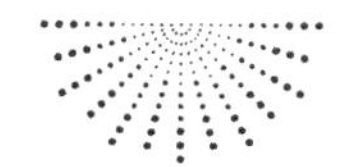

It wasn't long before Cherish and Favor were the last girls in the house. They'd had a bite to eat, and *Mamm* was packing a pie and some cake to take visiting. Cherish was rinsing the dishes they'd used. Because there was no work allowed on a Sunday, they usually let the dishes pile up until Monday morning.

"What's wrong with you?" *Mamm* asked suddenly.

"Nothing, I was just trying to be helpful, rinsing out the dishes so they won't be so hard to clean tomorrow."

"Not you. Not everything is about you, Cherish. I was talking to Favor."

Cherish looked over at Favor. Tears streamed down her face.

"It's just that I feel so unhappy. There's a gap in my life with Krystal gone, and now you're leaving me here with Cherish."

Cherish dried her hands. "We'll do something fun."

"I want to be with you, *Mamm*. Can I go with you and Levi today?" Favor asked in a whining tone.

Mamm put her arm around Favor. "Of course you can. Now dry those tears. The only thing is, you might get bored."

"*Nee,* I won't. I just want to be around people."

"I'm a person," said Cherish.

Mamm looked at Cherish. "Oh dear. That means you'll be all alone in the house by yourself. Would you like to come with us too?"

Cherish couldn't think of anything more dreadful than sitting around in Ada's stuffy living room with all the hundreds of embroidered scripture plaques everywhere. The upside was she always had plenty of chocolate cookies. "No, thank you, but you can bring back some of Ada's chocolate chip cookies if she has any to spare."

Mamm breathed out heavily. "*Nee.* I can't ask to bring cookies back."

"Why not? She knows I like them."

"We have the recipe. You can make yourself some tomorrow, but not today."

"They don't taste the same as how she makes them. I reckon she's got some secret ingredient she's left out of the recipe she gave us."

Favor laughed. "You're funny sometimes, Cherish."

"At least I made you smile."

"Are you ready, Favor?" *Mamm* asked.

Favor jumped up. "I'm ready."

Mamm walked to the door, then turned around to look at Cherish. "Are you sure you'll be all right by yourself?"

"I'm sure."

"What will you do?"

"I might just go for a walk through the orchard with Caramel. I might even say hello to Florence and Carter."

"That would be a good idea. That would make me feel better. I'm not sure I like you being home by yourself."

"I don't know why. I'm more than old enough."

"She'll be fine, *Mamm,* stop worrying."

"A mother always worries about her *kinner* no matter how old they are."

Cherish wiped her hands on the hand towel and followed them out of the room.

"Where is Levi?" *Mamm* looked around the living room.

Cherish opened the front door. "He's out there waiting for you already."

Favor walked up to Cherish. "Are you sure you don't mind me going?"

"Of course, I don't. You go and have fun. Eat some cookies for me."

Favor giggled. "I will."

A minute later, Cherish stood on the porch and waved them off. On her way back inside, she saw Caramel had found a cozy spot to sleep under the spare buggy in the barn.

With Caramel out of the way, it was Timmy's chance to use his wings. She rushed into the kitchen and then opened his cage door. He hopped onto her finger, and she lifted him out of his cage and set him on her shoulder. He went from one shoulder to the other, and then he flew off, heading for the kitchen sink. There, he perched on the faucet.

Cherish sat down in the chair. "Fly around, Timmy. There's no one to stop you. Now you can be free."

He then flew onto the kitchen table, then back onto the top of his cage. Then he worked his way down with his beak and his claws until he reached his door. To Cherish's surprise, he went back into the cage.

"What are you doing, Timmy? Do you like your cage that much?" He didn't answer. Instead, he moved his toy bell with his head. Cherish drummed her fingers on the table, wondering what she would do.

Once, when she was left alone in the house, she went through her mother's private papers and came across her father's will. That had changed their lives forever.

Wilma had deliberately hidden that will because it stated that *Dat* had left the orchard to Florence. *Mamm's* excuse was that Florence had left the community and had her father known that in advance, he would've changed his will.

There was just one little detail her mother had forgotten. At the time of his death, Florence was still in the community. She didn't leave until years later.

Everyone had forgiven *Mamm,* and her deception was shoved under the rug like so many other things.

That led Cherish to wonder... what else was in those private papers in *Mamm* and Levi's room?

She couldn't wait to find out. She left Timmy and walked upstairs.

Wilma and Levi's bedroom door was closed as it usually was, so she turned the handle and pushed it open.

When she was about to open the closet door to find the box of papers, she noticed a letter on the dresser.

She grabbed it and sat down to read it.

It was addressed to both her mother and Levi. And it was from a P Bruner. Cherish had no idea who that was.

Did this letter have anything to do with Debbie?

She carefully unfolded the one-page letter and read it.

DEAR LEVI AND WILMA,

I'm in desperate need of a solution to my problem. Pamela has taken ill and she'll be staying with her sister, who can take care of her. My long hours on the farm make it impossible for me to care for her.

That, however, is not the only problem in the family.

Debbie is now eighteen and we're finding things hard. Pamela and I are asking you to take Debbie in until we're in a better position. We wouldn't ask, but we don't know where else to turn. We will give you $100 a week for her keep, whether three months, six months, or one year. I wouldn't ask, but in one of Wilma's letters to Pamela, she mentioned that a girl was staying with you, and she left suddenly, leaving Wilma with a heavier workload.

This may work out well for both families.

Please call me, so we can discuss further.

Yours truly,

Peter

CHAPTER SEVEN

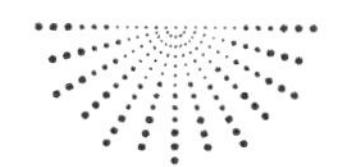

Cherish put the letter down. This girl was coming to them because *Mamm* had been complaining about having too much work. It was her fault.

Cherish spoke to herself. "Pamela must be Debbie's mother. If Debbie's eighteen, why can't she care for her mother? One hundred dollars to have Debbie staying here and she works in the house and the orchard? No wonder *Mamm* and Levi said yes to that."

Timmy flew in the door, giving Cherish a start. Then he landed on her head, but he relieved himself, just missing her face before he did so. She couldn't believe it when she looked down and saw the mess that had landed in the center of the letter.

"Timmy, see what you've done! Now I have to clean it." She stood up carefully, holding the paper by her fingertips. As soon as she did so, Timmy flew off. Cherish raced downstairs, carefully holding the letter.

She spread the letter out on the countertop and moistened some paper towels. She dabbed at the offending mess. Most of it came off, but now there was a dirty streak. All she could do was hope it looked better when it dried.

They wouldn't be home for hours.

While she had the letter on the sink, she raced up the stairs to get Timmy. She found him sitting on the windowsill, looking out. When she put her arm out in front of him, Timmy jumped onto it, and she walked downstairs with him.

"That was a very bad birdie. You go to the toilet in your cage so we can change the tray. You don't go anywhere you please; you don't."

When she got back in the kitchen, Timmy happily jumped into his cage, and she closed the door. She moved the letter closer, and re-read it.

"Why doesn't Debbie look after her mother, and why can't she stay at their farm? It's all strange if you ask me. They want to get rid of Debbie."

As much as Cherish felt sorry for Debbie because her mother was ill, she wasn't pleased about a stranger coming to live with them. But she soon felt better when she realized with Debbie here there'd be less work for her. Perhaps this could be Favor's new best friend to stop her whining all the time and clinging to *Mamm*.

CHERISH WAS SUDDENLY HUNGRY. She fixed herself a sandwich thinking some more about Debbie and Debbie's mother. Levi had told a very different story. Debbie's parents weren't separating if the woman was ill and had to move to her sister's. Why had Levi told them that?

An hour later, Cherish figured the letter was never going to look any better. It wasn't perfect, but it was a whole lot better now that it had dried a little. She pushed it back into the envelope and left it upstairs on the dresser just as she had found it.

Cherish grew tired and headed to her bed for a nap. She pulled the covers over her and pushed all her problems out of her mind.

"You've got a lot of explaining to do, my girl."

Cherish opened one eye to see her mother in her bedroom doorway with her hands on her hips. She must've been asleep for hours, and now they were all home. "What have I done now?"

"You let Timmy out of his cage."

Her other eye opened, and Cherish sat up. "Why would you say that?"

"Because he did his business on the kitchen floor far away from the cage."

Cherish's heart sank. He must've gone twice when he was out. At least she wasn't in trouble because she'd read the letter. Hopefully, they'd never find that out. "It's true. I'm sorry, *Mamm.*"

"No good being sorry, just clean it up."

"You left it there?"

"Yes. I left it there for you to clean up. Do you think that I should clean up after your bird? I don't even want it in the house. It's given me nothing but trouble." *Mamm* tapped her toe on the floor.

Cherish scrambled out of bed. "I'll do it right now."

"You'd better. Now hurry along before someone steps in it."

Cherish ran past her mother and continued down the stairs. She walked up to the mess, cleaned it away, and washed that section of the linoleum floor. Her mother came into the kitchen just as she was at the end of the project.

"And what have you been doing while I was away, apart from letting Timmy out of his cage?"

"Nothing much, I was tired, so I had a little rest."

"Is that all?"

Cherish looked over at her mother to determine if she knew she'd also read the letter. She didn't look angry enough for that. "Nothing all that interesting. There was no one here, so there wasn't much I could do without Favor. Where is she anyway?"

"She's helping Levi rub down the horse."

"That's good. Did you have a nice time with Ada and Samuel?"

"Jah denke, it was fine, a nice way to spend the afternoon."

"I bet Ada's looking forward to taking me to the farm."

"Yes, and so is Samuel. They haven't been there before, and they do like to travel. That's the benefit of not having an orchard. At their age, they are comfortably well-off, and they can come and go as they please. Levi and I are tied to the orchard because we're not as well-off."

"Strange they haven't been there before."

"They haven't been everywhere."

Cherish picked up the bucket and the mop and headed out the back door. She knew Levi had money tucked away somewhere. He had a lot of money out on loan to people in the community and had a few rental houses. They weren't poor like *Mamm* made out.

Cherish set the mop down and tipped the dirty water over Favor's vegetables. Extra nutrients for the beet plants. Thankfully, she didn't like beets. She rinsed the mop out in the bucket and left them to dry at the back door.

When she walked back inside, wiping her hands on her apron, she decided to take the opportunity of having her mother alone. Wilma was putting the teakettle on the stove.

"*Mamm,* what do you honestly think of Debbie coming here?"

"I think it's a fine idea. It worked out well with our last house guest, and she wasn't even one of us."

"I don't think it worked out well," Cherish said.

"We know exactly who Debbie is and exactly who her parents are."

"But is it really necessary that she stays here?"

"No, it's not necessary, but that's what Levi and I have decided. So there's no point trying to talk me out of it. You don't even know this girl. Why would you be so mean-spirited? The girl needs a home, and we have plenty of home to spare with all these bedrooms."

Her mother's words cut her deeply. She wasn't mean-spirited. They were such awful words. Worse than mean and even worse than selfish. Perhaps she was like that if her mother had said it. "Do you really think that of me?"

"Sometimes, I do. Some girls your age are uncaring because they haven't been through any of life's toils and hardships. Once you've been through a few hard times, you will learn some compassion."

Mother sat down at the table, and Cherish sat beside her. "I think I have been through some hard times."

Wilma looked at her. "Tell me what they were? I'd love to hear it."

"You and Florence sent me away to Dagmar's."

"And look how well that turned out for you."

"It did in the end, but I was crying all the way there the first time you sent me off. I just remembered her as a cranky old lady. We didn't get along immediately, you know. It took a few weeks before we got to understand each other. My point is, that was hard for me being away from my family, all alone at such a young age."

"Is that it?"

Her mother didn't understand her at all. Was there any use trying to share her feelings. "I've had some disappointments."

Mamm raised her chin. "Disappointments and hardships are two different things. You've always had a roof over your head, and you've always had enough to eat—"

"*Dat* died."

"*Jah,* that's true. That was hard for us all."

"Would you call that a hardship?"

Mamm looked down at the table. "I suppose I would."

"And then there was Levi. He was different when he first came here. Even you wanted to run away from home at one time."

Mamm put her hand over her mouth and giggled. "You do have a way with words. It did take us a while to adjust to one another. But it wasn't easy for him to come into an established family. It just wasn't like marrying a woman, and then you make a family. This family was already made, and he had to find his place in it."

"And he'd never run an orchard before."

"That's right."

When the kettle whistled, Cherish jumped up. "I'll get it for you, *Mamm.*"

"Denke, Cherish. I have a little surprise for you in the cupboard."

"Which cupboard?"

"The one where we keep the plates."

Cherish switched the gas stove off and then looked in the cupboard. On a white plate were two chocolate chip cookies. They were Ada's. There was no mistaking that. "You did get some from Ada."

"Jah. I asked her if I could take two cookies home to you. They were the last ones."

"Denke, Mamm, that's brightened my day immensely."

"And it will brighten my day immensely if you don't take too long to make my hot tea."

"It's coming." Cherish munched into one of the cookies.

CHAPTER EIGHT

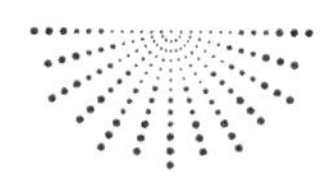

Much to Cherish's delight, the first day of Spring arrived. It was the day Ada and Samuel were accompanying Cherish to the farm.

Cherish had waited for this day for months. It was goodbye to chores, goodbye to worries, goodbye to annoying people, and hello to freedom—at least for a few days. While she was there, she would forget about her problems and everything that weighed her down.

She stood outside the house saying goodbye to everyone while Ada and Samuel waited in the car they'd hired. Samuel was in the front next to the driver, and Ada sat patiently, waiting for Cherish in the back.

Cherish had said goodbye to Timmy and made *Mamm* promise to be nice to him. She had also put two people in charge of feeding him and making sure he had fresh water, Bliss and Favor.

After she'd hugged everyone goodbye, she looked around for Caramel. This trip, she was leaving him home because Ada didn't want to be in the car on a long journey with a dog, she'd said.

"Come on, Cherish," Ada urged, with her body nearly halfway out the car window.

"I'm coming. I've just got to say goodbye to Caramel."

"The dog?" Ada squawked.

"Yes. I saw Caramel a moment ago, and now I can't find him." She called out his name a couple of times.

"*Ach,* don't worry. I'm sure he won't know you're gone," Ada called out from the car.

"He will. I must find him and say goodbye." Cherish walked back toward the house.

Ada stepped out of the car. "What now?"

"I have to look for Caramel."

"Are we going or not?" Cherish heard Samuel ask.

"It'll be fine, Cherish, just get in the car," *Mamm* said.

Levi just looked on like he didn't know what to say.

Her sisters stood there yawning, still looking as though they were half asleep.

Cherish knew she was risking a lecture when she ran into the house and sprinted up the stairs to her bedroom, but she couldn't leave without saying goodbye to her best friend and constant companion.

When she pushed the door open, she saw him on the bed with his head between his paws. She crouched down and hugged him. He'd seen her packing, and somehow he knew that he wasn't going too. He seemed sad and depressed, the way his big brown eyes looked up at her. "I'll miss you, but it'll only be for a few days. Everyone is going to look after you."

He licked her cheek, and she laughed. "Be good now, won't you?" Cherish hated leaving him with her mother, a dog hater, alone with him all day while the girls worked in the orchard.

"Cherish!" *Mamm* called out from downstairs.

"I'm coming," she yelled back. She kissed Caramel on the top of his head and then ran down the stairs. It wouldn't be the same without Caramel, but neither did she want to listen to Ada complaining about being cramped in the car with a dog.

As soon as the small talk stopped and Samuel's head had rolled to one side, indicating he was asleep, Cherish began her quest for obtaining more knowledge about Debbie. "Ada, what do you know of Debbie?"

"Debbie who?"

"Levi's niece. I'm not sure of her last name. Hold on a minute. Bliss said it was Levi's brother's daughter, so she must be a Bruner. Debbie Bruner."

"Oh, that's the girl who's coming to live with you?"

"Live? I thought she was only staying with us for a short time."

"You could be right."

"Anyway, what do you know about her?" Cherish asked.

"I heard that her mother and father are separating, moving into different houses. Oh, the shame that will bring. They most likely didn't want the poor girl living under that shadow. A new start is what they would want for her."

Cherish thought back to the letter. Levi and *Mamm* had

told Ada something different too. "Hmm. A new start in a different community."

"And Wilma and Levi are so welcoming. Debbie will be happy there, I'm sure. With so many girls, she's sure to make a good pal out of one of you."

"Well, she's coming to help out in the orchard. She won't be too comfortable."

"She comes from a farm, so she'd be used to hard work. Might show you girls how to do a proper day's work."

"What else do you know about her?"

"Like what?"

"Anything."

"That's all I've heard."

"Okay." Cherish looked out the window, disappointed.

After a long journey and many boring conversations with Ada giving her opinion about everyone in Cherish's family, and a few community members, they finally arrived at the farm.

Cherish looked out the window, hoping she'd find the farm in good condition. At least, find it how she'd left it. "Here we are. I'm so excited."

As they drove up the long driveway, Ada said, "You'll miss Caramel, I suppose."

"I know. I brought him here a couple of times. He loved playing with Dagmar's dogs."

"Are the dogs still here?"

"No, after she died, people in the community took

them. The bishop knew someone who wanted a couple of nice quiet dogs."

"That was good of him. It looks nice, Cherish. I thought it would be an old broken-down farmhouse. This is splendid, and oh so large."

Cherish was pleased to hear something positive. "You like it?"

"I do. Wake up, Samuel." Ada leaned over and shook Samuel's shoulder. "We are here. Wake up!"

He moved upright and looked around. "We're here already? That was fast."

"Only because you slept most of the way."

"Look at the house, Samuel, do you like it?" Cherish asked.

He stared out the window. "It's bigger than I expected. Is that yours there, Cherish?"

"Yes. That's it. You could have a bedroom each if you want to."

"That won't be necessary," said Ada. "It'll be a waste of time and only be more sheets to launder." Ada saw everything from a practical point of view.

"You can stop here," Samuel said to the driver. The driver did as he was told and then got out and proceeded to open the trunk to retrieve their luggage. After that, having already been paid, the driver turned the car around and headed back down the driveway.

"I wonder where Malachi is." Cherish picked up two suitcases.

A second later, Malachi charged out of the house. He was still the same, a complete mess. He was tall and thin and wearing un-ironed clothes. "You're here already? I wasn't expecting you till later tonight."

"We're here." Cherish said.

When Malachi took the bags from Cherish, Ada stepped forward.

"Malachi, this is Mrs. Berger, and Mr. Berger."

Ada swiped a hand through the air. "Just Ada and Samuel is fine."

Cherish smiled, knowing that if she hadn't introduced them that way, it wouldn't have been the right thing.

"Nice to meet you." Malachi nodded to Ada and then shook Samuel's hand. "Let's get everything inside." Malachi headed into the house with Samuel, who was carrying a large carton of food. Cherish and Ada walked along behind them.

"I can't wait to show you the place," Cherish told Ada.

"You can show me around tomorrow. I'm too tired to do any walking until then," Ada grumbled.

Once Ada and Samuel were shown to their room and had unpacked, they sat down in the living room with Malachi and Cherish.

"I'm cooking a nice dinner tonight for all of you," Malachi said.

"Oh, Malachi, we don't expect you to do that. I can make something. We brought food with us," Cherish said.

"I saw the food, and thank you. I want to cook for you. You've come all this way and you must be so tired."

"It's not that far. Samuel and I go much further than this, don't we, Samuel?"

"That's right, we do. Much further. We are taking

Cherish's mother up to see her new grandbabies, right to Wisconsin."

"It's not Wisconsin. It's Connecticut, Samuel. It's where my *schweschder* lives. She's your *schweschder*-in-law so you should remember it."

"Oh, well, it's just as far as Wisconsin, isn't it?"

"Possibly. I'm not sure. You should remember where my sister and her family live. You have been there countless times before." Ada sniffed the air. "I think I can smell dinner."

"Me too," said Samuel. "Is it a roast?"

"Yes."

"We'll look forward to it. We worked up an appetite on the journey. Samuel was asleep for most of the way," Ada said.

Samuel chuckled. "There's not much to do in the car, is there? We can't talk because there's the driver that we don't know."

"Cherish and I had a lovely talk in the back, didn't we, Cherish?"

"Yes, we did." Cherish smiled. The truth was, Ada talked, and all she did was listen.

When they heard a buggy, Malachi jumped up. "That'll be her now."

"Who?" Cherish asked.

"I've invited someone for the evening meal."

"Who is it?" Ada asked.

"I think you might've met her before, Cherish. It's Annie Whiley."

"Oh, is she still hanging around?" When Cherish realized how rude that sounded, she added, "I can't wait to see her again."

"That's good because she's looking forward to seeing you too." Malachi moved toward the door.

"We'll be pleased to meet some of your friends, Malachi. Is she more than a friend, hmm?"

Malachi laughed. "No, we're just friends. If you'll excuse me, I'll help her with the horse."

CHAPTER NINE

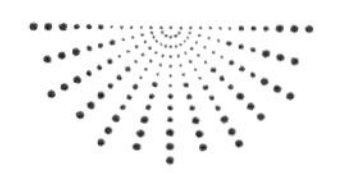

Once Malachi was outside, Cherish and Ada moved to the window to watch.

"I can tell you don't like this woman," Ada whispered softly enough so Samuel wouldn't hear them.

Cherish looked back at Samuel to see his eyes closed. "Was I that obvious?"

"I think you saved yourself with the second comment. Malachi wouldn't be aware you don't like her. Are you jealous, perhaps?"

Cherish drew her eyebrows together. "Jealous? Why would I be jealous of someone who is a practical stranger?"

"Do you mean practically a stranger?"

"Exactly. I wouldn't say I like Malachi. Not in the love kind of a way. I hope you don't think I do." Cherish looked back out the window. "I just don't see why they're friends." Annie was now smiling at Malachi, tossing her prayer *kapp* strings over her shoulder. "Why does he need a friend?"

Ada chuckled. "Would you like to be his only friend?"

"No, not at all. I suppose he should have some friends, some male friends. It's just that I thought he was a loner, you know? Living out here with no one else around for miles. Except for Ruth, and Rita and her husband on the other side."

"Yes, but they aren't of our faith, Cherish. He can't be friends with them, not close friends anyway."

"I wasn't saying that. They're too old anyway to be his friends, and he'd have nothing in common with them." Cherish looked out the window again. "This is dreadful."

Ada stared at her. "What's the matter now?"

"I was just looking forward to a relaxing dinner, and now I have to be polite."

"Oh, you weren't planning on being polite tonight? Good to know." Ada chuckled at her own words.

What was the use? Ada never understood how she felt and neither did *Mamm*. "I was planning on being polite. I'm always polite, aren't I?"

"Except when you're not. Now put a smile on your dial because they're heading toward the house. Make an effort to be friendly. When you move here, you'll need some people your own age. She could become a good friend to you."

"She's older," Cherish whispered.

"Not by much."

When Cherish saw them reaching the front door, she walked back to the couch. "With him here, I have to put up with strangers in my home."

Ada poked her in the ribs. "Shush, she'll hear you."

The door opened, and Annie walked in first. "Cherish, how are you?"

Cherish stood up and walked toward her. "Fine, thank you, Annie. Meet Ada and Samuel."

Samuel slowly opened his eyes and then sprang to his feet when he saw they had company.

Ada walked over and hugged Annie.

Then Cherish wondered if she, too, should've hugged Annie. It might have been polite, but the moment had passed. If she gave her one now, it would look like she was doing so because Ada had. "Do you live close by, Annie?" asked Cherish.

"I've moved closer since you were last here."

"Oh, that's simply wonderful," Ada said.

Annie smiled and looked up at Malachi. "I can spend more time with Malachi."

Cherish's heart sank. She didn't even like Malachi in that way, but she didn't want him involved with this woman. How much did he like Annie?

"Did you move there with your parents?" asked Ada.

"That's right." Annie turned around to face Malachi. "Oh, Malachi, I brought a pumpkin pie for dessert, and I left it in the buggy."

"Stay here. I'll fetch it." Malachi rushed out of the house.

Cherish raised her eyebrows. Now she was treating Malachi as though he worked for her. He didn't work for Annie; he worked for her.

"Let's sit by the fire," Ada said. "Would you like a cup of tea or coffee?"

"No, I just had one before I left."

Cherish wasn't looking forward to the next couple of hours. She wished she could wind the hands of the clock on to ten o'clock tonight. Annie would indeed be gone by then.

She had no idea what to say to this girl, and she didn't want to have a polite conversation. All she wanted was to think about her farm and talk to Malachi about it. Now she was worried that Malachi would get into a relationship with Annie, and then his farm duties would slide.

During dinner, things only got worse. Ada and Annie got on wonderfully. The conversation had somehow gotten around to gingerbread.

"My mother makes the most amazing gingerbread houses. She sells them to the local store at Christmas time. And do you know what?"

Ada leaned forward. "What?"

"They always sell out of them. I often help, and we can't make enough of them. My mother decorates them so well, all out of sugar frosting. She makes little people as decorations and everything."

Cherish didn't like Annie getting all the attention. "We had a gingerbread house at Christmas one time."

"I can't remember that," Ada said.

"We did."

"Ada, my mother is making some tomorrow. Would you like to watch? I'll be there helping her."

"I'd love that."

"What about you, Cherish? Would you like to come too?" Annie asked.

"No, Cherish is here to see about the farm. If we had more time, she could take a more leisurely approach."

"Thanks for your offer, Annie, but Ada's right. Sometime, I'd love to see how the gingerbread houses are made."

Samuel said, "I love gingerbread. Is it all right if I watch too?"

Ada shook her head. "No, Samuel, you'll be here helping give Malachi some pointers about farming."

Malachi sat straight in his chair. "I don't need any. I've been running this farm by myself for some time. Before that, I ran other farms."

Samuel smiled. "That's settled then."

Ada stared at Malachi. "So, you don't think you could improve on anything at all? This place is perfect, is it?"

Malachi sat up straight and looked Ada directly in the eyes. "I suppose there's always room to improve something."

"Exactly. Samuel will help you do that."

"I can do that anytime. We're here for a few days, Ada. I really am a fan of gingerbread, and it'd be a real treat to watch a house being made."

Ada sighed. "It's more of a ladies thing. I don't think Annie's father will be there, will he, Annie?"

"No, he won't. He died last year."

Cherish was immediately sorry for Annie. They had something in common. They'd both lost their fathers. "I'm sorry to hear that, Annie. My father died too."

"Thank you, and I'm sorry about yours."

Ada looked down for a moment and then said, "So if you go, Samuel, you'll be the only man there."

Cherish looked over at Annie to see if she'd be shocked by Ada. She didn't offer any sympathies to Annie about her father. Ada could've at least said something, but no, she never said anything, just kept talking, trying to stop Samuel from going too.

Ada said to Samuel. "Once I see how they're made, I'll make one, and you can watch me make it."

Samuel smiled. "Okay. I'll have to be happy with that."

"I'll make one as soon as we get home. As long as they're not too difficult. Do you think I could learn the art of gingerbread-house-making in one day, Annie?"

"Definitely."

"Wunderbaar." Ada clapped her hands together.

For the next few moments, everyone kept quiet while they ate.

CHAPTER TEN

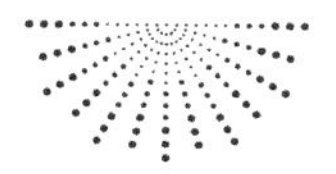

The next day, Samuel borrowed Malachi's buggy to drive Ada to Annie's house. Samuel showing Malachi what to do on the farm would have to wait for another day.

Malachi and Cherish stood there and watched them drive away.

"Poor Samuel. He wanted to be involved so bad," Malachi said. "Now he has to drive her there and to do what? Wait in the buggy?"

Cherish burst out laughing. "I'd say he'd come back here and fetch her later."

"No, he can't. It's too far. Ada sure is bossy."

"I know. Samuel doesn't seem to mind. I think it's come on gradually. I don't remember her being like that when I was younger."

"I'll show you around so you can see what I've done since the last time you were here."

"Okay. I can't wait to see everything."

"Let's go up to the top of the hill, and we can look

down on the whole farm." As they walked, Malachi grabbed a reed and stuck it in his mouth. "I can't tell you how excited I was when you told me that Ada and Samuel were bringing you."

"You wanted to meet Ada and Samuel?"

He chuckled. "You know that's not what I mean. I told you in my letters that I enjoy our talks."

Cherish didn't know what to say, so she didn't say anything.

"I like the conversations we have," he repeated as though she hadn't heard.

"Yes, I know, but can't you talk to Annie?"

"I do talk to her. She's a good friend, but she's not you."

"No, she's not me. She's Annie."

"I meant it when I said that she and I are just friends and nothing more. I don't want you to get the wrong idea about that."

"I believed that when you said it the first time. Why do you feel the need to keep saying it? Is that because it's not true?"

"You're a hard woman to please, Cherish."

She couldn't help but smile; no one had ever referred to her as a woman. She was always a girl, just a silly girl. That's what she was back home, and she was sure that's how everyone thought of her. The youngest, the spoiled one, and the one who talked too much. "Not really. I do like to talk. It's better to talk than to have silence, don't you think?"

"Silence is okay sometimes."

"Silence is boring."

"And you're anything but boring." He glanced at her, and she knew he was admiring her, and it felt good to be appreciated.

"Thank you." She didn't know if that was a compliment or not. Maybe he liked boring people if Annie was his friend. Then Cherish felt a little bad for thinking mean things about Annie because Annie had always been lovely. But while she was nice on the outside, was Annie thinking mean thoughts about her? Maybe Annie went home and told her mother how she disliked this girl called Cherish, who owned the farm Malachi worked on.

"What are you thinking, Cherish?"

"Nothing much."

"You said you don't like silence, and then you were silent just now. I reckon you were talking to yourself, silently, in your head."

"Well, I can't be talking one hundred percent of the time, can I? Why don't you say something?"

"I don't know if you'll like what I've got to say."

Cherish stopped and looked at him. "What is it?" If he was working up to declaring his undying love to her, better to get it over with, and then she could tell him she wasn't interested. Better that news comes sooner rather than later. It would clear the air. When he hesitated for too long, she said, "Look, Malachi, I like you, but I just don't see a future for the both of us."

He looked at her, and then the corners of his eyes crinkled before he laughed. "You think I like you in that way?"

"Don't you?"

"No. I like you as a friend. Liking you as anything else never entered my head."

Cherish looked down, feeling like a fool, until she remembered the letters. She looked back up at him. “You’re always saying in your letters about missing me and stuff, so I don’t think it was unreasonable of me to think what I thought.”

“I do, but I was never thinking anything romantic.”

Cherish huffed. “Now, I feel stupid. Good to know I’m so unappealing.”

“You’re not. It’s nothing like that.”

“What’s it about?” Cherish asked.

CHAPTER ELEVEN

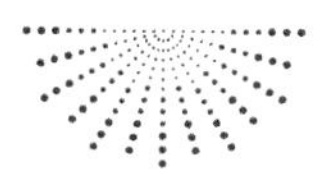

"It's about the barn," Malachi said.

"The barn?" This was not what she expected. He was supposed to say he was in love with her or something similar. His letters indicated he liked her; she was sure of it. Disappointment rippled through her. It was a nice feeling to have someone like her, and now he didn't. Those thoughts left her, quickly replaced by worry about the barn. "What's wrong with the barn?"

"It needs repair, and there's nothing in the budget for it."

"That's no problem. Just sell something to cover the cost."

"Exactly what would you like me to sell? We need all the animals to produce income. I don't think we have anything to sell. I had a good clean out after I arrived, and anything that could be sold, I sold for materials to upgrade the fences."

Cherish frowned. She recalled some fences had needed some repair. "How much will it cost?"

"Two hundred for the lumber. I can get people out to help, but that's what the materials will cost."

"Just get cheaper materials, then."

He tipped his hat back slightly. "It's the whole back of the barn that needs replacing, Cherish. If we use cheaper materials, we'll be needing to do it all again in a year or two. I'm not used to doing shoddy work. Don't make me do it."

"Okay, let me think about it for a day or two."

"I just hope it will last out through the snow."

"We won't be having any snow until the end of the year. We're coming into the warm weather."

He shook his head. "I know, but I'm hoping when ya say you'll think about it for a day or two, it don't end up being months."

She stopped herself from correcting his words. "You shouldn't have left it until the last minute to tell me about it. You shouldn't be just bringing things up to me like this. This is the kind of thing you need to tell me about in your letters."

"Only just found out about it as well."

Cherish bit her lip so she would not say something rude. "This is just another thing, another problem just when I thought I could deal with all my problems then this is just..." Cherish took a deep breath and tried to hold back tears.

"You look like you're about to cry. What's the matter?"

"I'm entitled to cry if I choose to do it."

"Sure, cry if you want. I only want to know what's wrong with ya. What are these problems you're talking about?"

Cherish took a deep breath. "Let's sit down somewhere, and I'll tell you."

He whipped off his coat, moved a couple of paces and spread it down in front of a clump of trees. "These trees will serve as a windbreaker."

"Thank you. Aren't you cold?" She stared at his thin shirt.

"No."

Cherish sat down cross-legged and covered her legs with her long dress. "This is where I need my dog. Caramel would cuddle up to me and keep me warm. But it's not that cold out of the wind."

He sat down beside her with his legs straight out. "Unburden yourself. Tell me all ya problems."

"Are you sure?"

"Sure, I'm sure."

She'd already touched on some things in her letters, so she told him the rest of the story about Caroline turning out not to be Caroline and being someone else entirely, and that same girl had let slip to a reporter about Wilma's secret. Because she trusted Malachi, she told him what that secret was. Then she talked about what Daniel, the reporter, had threatened. "So, what do you think about all that?"

He rubbed his face. "Well, I can see why you're so upset."

"It is bad? Everyone is trying to tell me it's not bad, but it is. I knew it was."

"Well, I wouldn't be happy about it. It's not right. It's just not right."

"I know that. But it's something that can't be fixed.

Everyone is telling me not to worry about it. Earl even came from Ohio to talk to the reporter, and he didn't have any luck with him."

"What's this reporter's name?"

"He's Daniel Whitcombe. He was Daniel Withers, but he changed his name."

"Which is it then?"

"Whitcombe."

"I'll remember that. Where does he work?"

Cherish gave him the name of the newspaper.

"And why is he so keen to tell these stories?" Malachi asked.

Cherish shrugged. "Desperation I guess. He's very competitive—very driven to succeed. He's tired of all the silly stories the paper is giving him, and he wants to do deeper stories. He needs a breakthrough. I think that's where he's coming from."

"If the paper gives him silly stories, sounds like they don't think much of him."

Cherish leaned over and grabbed a ripe dandelion. "He's only starting out. I think that's how they treat all the new reporters."

"I think this guy needs to change his mind and change it quickly."

"Me too. If he decides to do it, no one will be able to stop him." She blew on the dandelion seeds, but the wind was going the wrong way, and they came back on her.

"I think I'll be able to find a way."

Cherish brushed off the dandelion remnants, knowing Malachi wouldn't be able to do a thing. "But he didn't listen to Earl, so what do you think you can do?"

"Just leave it with me."

He was a simple farm boy. He couldn't speak like they did where she was from, and his handwriting was much worse than his spoken words. There'd be nothing he could do to discourage Daniel or stop him. "Thanks, Malachi. I appreciate the thought."

"No need to appreciate the thought, appreciate the job when it's been completed. I'm pretty sure, no, I'll guarantee I'll fix this guy for you."

He was so severe it made her laugh. "I will appreciate it when it's done."

"And I'll need somethin' in return."

She held her breath. He was going to try to steal a kiss. "And what's that?"

"The barn will need to be fixed as soon as possible."

"And that's what you want in return?" Did he forget it was her farm?

"That's right. Are you sure you're not cold?"

Maybe she read his signals wrong. Perhaps he thought of her as just a friend, same as he thought of Annie. She wrapped her arms around herself. "I'm not cold at all. What about you?"

He looked over the green fields. "A little, but I like the outdoors. I prefer to be cold under the blue sky than being warm sittin' at home. What about you?"

"I'm the same."

"Do you think you'll ever sell this place, Cherish?"

"No, never. Aunt Dagmar never would've sold, so I'm not going to sell either."

"She's gone now, and she wouldn't want you to be burdened with this place. Are ya having trouble paying for the repairs? If you are, you've got to be practical."

"Everything will work out. I'll come up with the money. I'll always keep this place. It's mine. I've never really had anything that's mine and mine alone apart from my dog, Caramel, and Aunt Dagmar's bird, Timmy."

"And how is Timmy?"

"He sends his regards."

Malachi chuckled. "I'll bet he does. You know I don't do well with birds."

"I thought your only phobia was chickens."

"Birds are similar, but you're right. The phobia is only for chickens. I just don't like birds."

Cherish shook her head. "You'd get along great with my mother."

"How is Wilma?"

"I forgot you met her. She's okay. I'll tell her you were asking about her."

"If you must."

"I must. She likes it when people ask about her. I can't believe you freely admit to having a phobia."

"Hey, I don't label it. You're the one who did that."

"You agreed with me."

"It's easier to agree with you. Anyway, sometimes I can't get a word in edgeways."

"Speaking about Timmy, Miriam said he needs another bird for companionship."

He laughed. "Yeah, I'd reckon it's true. Everyone needs someone." He stared at her and made her feel uncomfortable.

"Yes, well, *Mamm* is always complaining that he chirps

too much, and Miriam said he wouldn't do that so much if he had a friend."

"Maybe it's the same with you. You wouldn't talk so much if you had a friend."

She glared at him. "You want me not to talk to you, is that it?"

He laughed again. "I'm teasing you. So, are you getting another bird?"

"No. *Mamm* hates animals, especially ones that live in the house. I've never understood people who don't like animals. What about you?"

He rubbed his chin. "Yeah. I think we're here to be caretakers of the animals, among other reasons. Make sure we do our best to look after 'em."

She smiled, loving his answer.

CHAPTER TWELVE

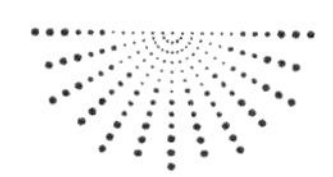

Later that day, Cherish was a little shocked to see Annie back again.

She arrived at the same time as Ada and Samuel.

Cherish and Malachi were looking out the window when they saw the second buggy.

Cherish said, "Annie's here again. We should've thought about dinner. She'll be staying, I'd say."

"That's okay. There are plenty of leftovers from last night to heat up."

"Are you sure?"

"Yes."

Cherish looked out the window again and saw that Samuel was walking behind Ada and Annie. "Malachi, I think Samuel is carrying a gingerbread house. I thought they were only for Christmas or something. People just don't have them for dessert, do they? Or is that what they do around these parts?"

"We're the same as your community, Cherish. We're not that different."

"I think you're different here."

"Not so different that we have gingerbread houses for dessert." He shook his head.

"Well, how do I know that's not what you do?"

"It'd be silly, wouldn't it?" he asked.

Cherish laughed. "I can't wait to tell Annie what you said."

"Don't you dare tell her that gingerbread is silly. She mightn't be pleased with you."

"Or with you. You're the one who said it, and she might not like you anymore."

"That's not what I mean," he called after Cherish as she hurried to open the front door for them.

Ada didn't say hello. All she said was, "I've invited Annie again for the evening meal."

Cherish said, "That's good. I'm so glad you could come, Annie. We'll only be having leftovers from last night's meal if that's all right?"

"That's wonderful. I really liked what we had."

Cherish looked at what Samuel had in his arms. It was covered by a white cloth. "Is that a gingerbread house?"

"Yes, we brought it to show you," said Annie.

"You brought it to show me?"

"Yes, you and Malachi. It's not for eating. It's entered in the local show. My mother just has to make a few adjustments, but this is what will be entered. She always wins first prize."

Malachi rushed to hold the door open for Samuel to fit through with the large gingerbread house.

"Set it on the kitchen table, Samuel. That way, we can all admire it," Malachi said.

"*Mamm* wins first prize every year for the novelty section."

"There's a show around here?" Cherish asked.

"It's only five miles away."

"When?"

"At the end of the month."

"Oh, we'll be back home by then. I hope your mother wins."

"She will."

When dinnertime rolled around, Cherish and Malachi went into the kitchen to heat up the food. Cherish left Malachi to do it while she sat staring at the gingerbread house. After clanging pots and pans and turning on the gas stove, Malachi sat next to her.

"What are you thinking, Cherish?"

"I want to hate it, but I can't."

He burst out laughing. "Why would you want to hate it?"

"Because it's all annoying how Ada's so interested in making these now."

She put her finger on the hard-white-frosting snow on the roof.

"Careful. I don't think you should be touching it."

Cherish lowered herself so she'd be level with the windows. She looked inside the windows and saw two figures. "Oh! I don't believe it."

"What?"

"There are people inside."

"What? She didn't say anything about that."

He bumped Cherish on the shoulder so she'd move over. When she did, he looked inside. "That's pretty clever if you ask me."

"It is pretty, and it does smell all gingery, and it's colorful." Then Cherish realized how close she was to Malachi. He must've realized at the same time, too because he cleared his throat and moved a few inches away.

The meal with Annie was easily as boring as the last night's dinner. Cherish wasn't pleased because she was only at the farm for five days, and Annie had taken up too much of her time.

Cherish was pleased that Annie left right after the meal and took her gingerbread house with her.

CHAPTER THIRTEEN

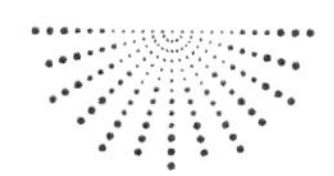

Cherish woke early and quickly started the task of changing into her day clothes. She didn't want to miss one moment of being at her farm. Sleep was such a waste at times like these.

When she'd pulled on her dress, stockings, and apron, she unbraided her hair and ran a brush through it. Every night, she fashioned her long hair into a loose braid to save it from tangles. After one hundred strokes, she divided her hair into two sections, as Dagmar had shown her. She braided the sections and then wound the two braids onto her head in a circle, fastening them with pins. Lastly, she popped on her prayer *kapp.*

She then hurried out the door to get a head start on the day. When she got to the kitchen, she found everyone was already awake and sitting at the table, looking like they'd been awake for hours. It was only just before six. "Oh, this is a surprise."

Ada turned around from the stove. "I was just about to come and get you. Take a seat."

Cherish sat down between Samuel and Malachi. "Good morning, everyone. I was going to make breakfast."

"You slept in," said Samuel, in a voice that was way too loud for her morning ears to tolerate.

"Yes, it seems like it."

"We need more bread," Ada announced as she served fried eggs and bacon onto four plates.

"We could drive to the store and get some," said Samuel. "There's a store around somewhere, isn't there, Malachi?"

"Sure is. Out the driveway, turn left, keep going for five miles, and you'll find the store on this road. It's only small. Blink, and you'll miss it."

"Seems everything is five miles from here," Cherish said.

"Could we borrow your buggy today, Malachi? Samuel and I talked about it, and we wouldn't mind looking around the neighborhood either before we visit your uncle, Bishop Zachariah." Ada placed a full plate down in front of Malachi and another in front of Samuel.

"I don't mind at all. Use it whenever you want. Only thing is, don't worry about buying any bread. I'll bake some today."

"A man baking?" Ada cackled. "Never heard such a thing."

"He has to do everything, Ada. He lives on his own," Cherish said. "He'd starve otherwise."

"Very sad." Ada set Cherish's plate down in front of her and sat down to one herself.

"Thanks for this, Ada. It looks delicious," Cherish said. "I might sleep in more often."

Malachi and Samuel agreed that the food looked good, and then they all closed their eyes for their silent prayers of thanks.

When they opened their eyes, Cherish said, "I can help you make the bread, Malachi."

"Okay. I won't say no. I should've made more knowing that ya'll were comin,' but things got away from me."

"Cherish is good at anything she sets her mind to," Ada said. "I'm sure your bread is nice, Malachi, but Cherish might be able to show you how to make it better."

"Thank you, Ada," Cherish said. "That's encouraging."

"It's true."

Malachi finished his mouthful and said, "I'd be grateful for the help, Cherish. I never had someone show me how to cook. I just figured it out from following the recipe cards in the box in the cupboard."

Cherish nearly dropped the fork she'd just picked up. "You look after those. They're Dagmar's."

"They're yours now, Cherish." Samuel's voice was just as loud as before.

Cherish was pleased she wasn't sitting next to him.

Now Ada had to have her say. "You're right, Samuel, but I don't know why they weren't left to all Wilma's girls." She stared at Cherish. "Just like the farm should've been left to all your siblings and your half-siblings."

Cherish ate a mouthful of toast as she debated whether to tell Ada it wasn't her fault. She had no idea that Dagmar had planned to leave her the farm.

"I'm sure Cherish's aunt would've considered all the options," Samuel said.

Cherish looked down at her food as she cut open the egg. It was embarrassing for Ada and Samuel to be talking about these things in front of Malachi.

"It was God's will that Cherish have the farm," Malachi said.

Cherish wasn't brave enough to look up, but at least that put an end to Ada's talk. *Mamm* had been most upset when she'd learned Cherish had inherited the farm. She was the one who had said it should've been left to all Dagmar's nieces and nephews. "You see, Dagmar only really knew me. That's why she did what she did."

"Nonsense. She saw all of you a few times. And why should she have to know the people? These people are her blood, part of her."

Cherish had to stand up for herself and Dagmar. "Before I was sent away to come here, I only remember meeting her the once."

"I'm sure it was more than that, wasn't it, Samuel?"

Everyone looked at Samuel.

He shrugged his shoulders. "Possibly." This time his voice wasn't so loud.

Cherish decided she had to go further in defending Dagmar's decision, especially since they were in Dagmar's house. "We got on really well together. She was like my other mother, so—"

Ada gasped. "I hope you've never said that to your poor *mudder.*"

"*Nee.* I wouldn't, but *Mamm* knows how close we became."

"She was playing favorites and I don't like the idea of it. I've never done that and I don't think it's right."

"Dagmar didn't see it like that. She wanted to keep the farm going and she knew that I loved it as much as she did. Anyway, it was her decision, so that is that."

Samuel said, "I don't think we should be talking about this. Cherish is right. What's done is done. It was Dagmar's decision to make, and she made it. Like it or loathe it, that's what she decided. It was her farm, now it belongs to Cherish, and I think that gave Dagmar a certain satisfaction."

Cherish put her head down and kept eating. She didn't need to look up. She could feel the steam coming out of Ada's ears. It was rare that Samuel disagreed with her. Ada was quiet now, but when they got into the buggy and were alone, Cherish was certain that Samuel would get an earful.

CHAPTER FOURTEEN

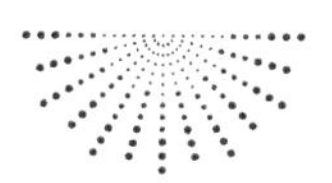

An hour later, Cherish felt relief flow through her body when Ada and Samuel finally left for their outing. She stood next to Malachi on the porch as they watched the horse and buggy leave.

"You can help me feed the animals," he said.

"I'd love to, but don't forget about the bread."

"I won't. We can do that after."

They headed to the barn and, as Malachi began dividing the hay bales into slices, Cherish blurted out, "I just want to let you know that if you marry Annie, I can't let you both stay here at the farm."

He stopped what he was doing and turned to face her. "You're firing me?"

"So you do intend to marry her?"

"I didn't say that."

Cherish had to find out more about their relationship. "You kind of did... just as well as."

"I thought I was staying here looking after the farm

until ya got 'ere. I didn't know you'd put restrictions on me."

"Yes, *you* stay here, not anybody else, and only if you're doing a good job."

He put one hand against the wall and leaned on it. "Aren't I doing a good job?"

"I guess so."

He stared at her with his eyes wide open.

"Don't look at me like that. Okay, you are doing an okay job."

"Thanks, Cherish, that's all I wanted to hear." The corners of his lips turned upward.

"You're missing the point."

"You made your point and I heard it. I've got no intention of marrying Annie any time soon, but I think if I wanted to, I should and still stay here. I've put a lot into this place. It's been my life. I was planning on moving' only when you get here for good."

"You're so frustrating and confusing, Malachi. You say one thing, and then you say another."

He stood up straight and the slight smile left his lips. "No, I'm not confused at all. I haven't said one thing different. Tell me what I've said that's confusing."

"There would be no need to be upset about it if you haven't thought about marrying her."

"That's what has ya worried?" He chuckled. "If I didn't know you any better, Cherish Baker, I think you were jealous."

"I am not. I'm not jealous of anybody and never have been. Jealousy is something that doesn't serve a purpose."

She'd had to think quickly, and she said what she thought Ada would say. For Ada, everything had to have a purpose.

He yawned and then covered his mouth. "Excuse me."

"Am I keeping you awake?" she asked.

"I'm sorry, I didn't get much sleep last night."

Neither had she, thanks to Samuel's loud snoring. "Too busy thinking about Annie?"

He laughed. "You don't give up easily, do you. I told you, we're just friends, no need to be jealous." He gave her a wink.

"You're just the same as most men I've met. Disappointing."

He threw his head back and laughed. "Why are men so disappointing?"

"Eddie the beekeeper was so in love with Caroline and then when she turned out to be Krystal—"

"Yeah, well, she lied. Don't blame 'im one bit."

Cherish shook her head. "She said she was sorry. Everyone makes mistakes. He should look past that."

"Nope. She ruined his trust. What else you got?"

"Adam, Bliss's boyfriend. He didn't like her until he got a letter. The letter was from me."

"I don't think I've heard this story. Continue."

"Don't give me a lecture about it. I already feel bad enough. She was sending him a letter, and I swapped it out to put myself in a better light with him. It totally backfired on me."

"Wait a minute. Wind back a bit. You said things in the letter about yourself, pretending it was Bliss who was writing?"

"Yes, I replaced her letter with one of my own. I wrote the letter as Bliss saying something good about myself."

He burst out laughing and then doubled over. After a while, he straightened up. "That's so wrong. I don't know why I find it so funny."

"It wasn't funny at all. He came back because he fell in love with the person who wrote it. He thought he was in love with Bliss, but he was really in love with me. When he found out the truth some weeks later, he'd already fallen in love with Bliss for real." Cherish sighed. "It's just not fair. He should be in love with me." She regretted saying that last bit as soon as she said it.

His eyes narrowed. "You're a little young."

"Yeah, well, Bliss isn't that much older."

"So for those two reasons alone, you think men are dreadful? Correct me if I'm mistaken, but weren't you deceptive in both of those examples?"

"No." When he kept staring at her, she added, "Well, maybe with Eddie because I was telling him how to act and everything and what to say, but in the other case with Adam… oh, I see what you mean."

"My mother would say you stick your nose into other people's business."

She turned around and walked away. Over her shoulder, she said, "I think we should get back to the house."

He followed her. "Not yet, I'm not done talking."

She spun around. "Let's not talk about this anymore. I don't want to argue."

"Suits me. Ya going to help with some chores?"

"Of course. It's my farm. You're helping me. Just remember that."

"Whichever way ya want to look at it, just let's do it."

They spent the next three hours working on the farm, and Malachi introduced her to his new routines.

It was so close to lunchtime that Cherish's tummy rumbled. "Oh did you hear that?"

"What?"

"My stomach. I'm hungry, and we should get back to the house to make something for Ada and Samuel. They should be back soon."

"I doubt it. They'll be out for ages. They said they'd visit my uncle. He lives a fair distance away. I'm sure my aunt will feed them lunch. Are you hungry?"

"You have no bread left. We should bake some bread now. I mean, I should bake some. Your bread is a bit hard. I don't know what you're doing to it, but it should be soft. Fresh bread is always warm and soft, and it smells delicious."

"My bread not up to standard, eh?"

She smiled at him. "Not really."

"You reckon you're a better bread maker?"

"Anyone would be." She looked over at a cow. "That cow would be a better bread maker."

He laughed. "I can see I ain't going to get anything past you."

"What would you be trying to get past me?"

"No, nothin'. It's just an expression." He raised his hands up in the air. "Relax."

"If you say so. If you want me to relax, just say stop saying stupid things and iron your clothes once in a while, and bake some decent bread."

He laughed. "How about you show me the proper way to make bread?"

"You mean no one's ever shown you before?"

"Nah, I'm just following the recipes in your aunt's recipe box."

Cherish shook a finger at him. "You better be looking after those."

"You told me that already and I have been. All I'm doing is reading 'em. Will reading them wear 'em out?"

"No."

"That's all I'm doing,'"

Cherish knew she was giving him a hard time, but she couldn't stop. "I'll show you how to make proper bread, and it will be the nicest you've ever tasted. Well, it might not be that good. It'll still be a lot better than yours."

"Can't wait."

"Let's go."

CHAPTER FIFTEEN

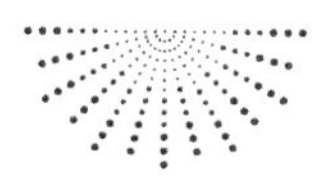

As they walked to the house, Malachi said, "Not all men are the same. Take me, for example. I'll be a good catch for some girl or woman."

Cherish smiled, trying to contain her laughter. "Why's that?"

"I'm polite, considerate, and thoughtful. I have a lot of love to give the right woman when that day comes, and I'll look after her like she's somethin' special."

"That sounds lovely. I'm sure the two of you will be very happy together." As long as you don't think you'll be happy together on my farm, Cherish thought.

"What you need to do is stop sticking your nose in. No wonder nothing has worked out for you."

Cherish was hurt by his comment. "Don't you say that. Good things happen to me all the time. I met Dagmar, and we became close before she died. Now I have her farm. Those were good things."

"I meant with men. You'll not have any success with

them when you're older if you keep messing in people's lives. No one wants a woman like that." He shook his head.

"Number one, you have the wrong idea about me. Number two, you're not my father or my brother, so keep your ideas to yourself."

"Number three?"

"Number three, don't be so annoying and judgmental."

He shrugged his shoulders. "Fair call."

Once they were in the kitchen, Cherish opened all the cupboards to see what food was where.

"I'll get the bread tins and turn on the stove." Malachi bent down and rattled around the saucepan cupboard.

"I don't suppose you use a bread starter."

He looked up at her. "A bread what?"

"Never mind. I know a different way to make it. I'll need a large bowl to mix all the ingredients." Cherish gathered everything together.

He was still trying to find the bread tins. "I couldn't find a recipe card for bread, so I went to the library and wrote down the recipe."

"You have a library around here?"

"No. It was a mobile library that comes around every three months. Got 'em," he said, holding up two loaf tins.

"Okay, put them near the stove."

"What now?"

"We dissolve the sugar in some warm water."

He looked at all the ingredients. "How do I know how much of each thing?"

"I'll write it down for you later. Seeing that you can read."

"Very funny."

"Here. You stir it." He took over from her.

"Tell me when the sugar has all gone."

"Looks to be all gone now."

"Okay, now we stir in the yeast. Then we allow it to proof until it foams."

"It's similar to what I do," Malachi said.

Cherish rolled her eyes. "It's obviously not what you do, and you'll taste the difference once it's ready to eat."

When it became foamy, she had him stir the oil and the salt into it. "Now mix the flour in slowly."

"Okay."

"While you're doing that, I'll make a floured surface so we can knead it."

He mixed in the flour a little at a time, until it was fairly stiff and held together, and then she showed him how to knead. "Not too much," she added. "Or it will be tough."

"Maybe that's what I was doing wrong."

"Could be. Now we put a little oil into the pans. I'll quickly do that now." When she'd done that, she had him put the mixture into the two pans. "Now we cover it with a damp cloth and leave it near the oven to rise. It'll double in size in about an hour."

"A whole hour. What'll we do until then?"

"We can clean up this mess." She put her hands on her hips and looked around the clutter filled kitchen. "What I mean is *you* can clean up this mess."

He grabbed the floured board. "Is that right?" Then he put two fingers in the flour and dabbed some on her nose. He doubled over, laughing. "You should see yourself."

She wasn't going to let him get away with that. Her hands went straight to the leftover flour. Then she gave chase as he ran out of the house.

In no time, he was in the middle of the fields, and then he turned around. She had nearly caught up to him. "I didn't know you were such a fast runner. Must be all the boys you're running away from, or could be running to."

She charged forward, and he turned to run again, but he tripped and toppled over. Cherish took the opportunity and got close enough to spread some flour over his face.

"Okay, okay, you win." He sat up. "You got me."

She sat on the ground with him, wiping the flour from her nose.

"What if I was badly hurt when I fell just now?" he asked.

"I knew you weren't."

He brushed the flour off his cheeks. "All gone?"

She leaned forward and wiped it with her fingertips. Just for fun, she left some on. "That's better. What about me? All gone?" she asked.

"Yes."

Cherish could tell he had hurt himself because he'd landed with such a thud. "Are you sure you haven't broken anything?"

"I'm fine."

"How will you know unless you get up and try to walk?"

"I didn't hear a crunch or a snap. That's what broken bones do."

"Not always."

"So, you're an expert on broken bones too?"

"Yes, and bruises. I can tell how long a person's had a bruise by the color."

He shook his head. "I won't even ask." Then he leaned back on his hands. "I'm glad you've come here, Cherish."

"Me too."

"And I'm glad we cleared the air about that other thing. I only like you as a friend."

"Oh, me too."

"You're a fun person to have around."

She smiled and then looked away, a little disappointed that he didn't like her. What was wrong with her? Did she have to make gingerbread houses for him to be fonder of her?

"What'll we do about the bread?"

"Leave it for a while. It's got to rise, don't forget."

"That's right. You said that. Why have you gone quiet all of a sudden? You look miserable."

"I'm thinking about Bliss." She wasn't thinking about her at all, but she had to say something. It wasn't as though she could tell him she was upset that he didn't like her even though she didn't like him either. That would sound crazy.

"Bliss, she's your half-sister, right?"

"Nope, she's my stepsister. She's doing my shift at the café for me, and I'm hoping it all goes well for her."

"I'm sure she'll be fine. Forget about home while you're here. You said you've been looking forward to it all year. Exactly what parts were you most looking forward to apart from seeing me again?"

She hit him on the arm for being cheeky. “Seeing what you’ve done."

"Let’s go for a walk, and I’ll show you all the fence repairs I’ve done.” He stood.

“Are you joking right now?”

“No.” He grabbed her hand and pulled her to her feet. Once she was standing, she snatched her hand away.

“Life on the farm isn’t as exciting as you seem to think.”

She placed her hands on her hips. “I stayed here with Dagmar for long enough to know what it’s like.”

“Okay, but I think it’s pretty mundane. Sometimes I don’t see a living soul for days.”

“I know. I’ve lived here.”

“Yeah, with Dagmar, not by yaself.”

Glancing back at the house, she said, “We should wait for the bread first. And after it’s in the oven, we can’t go too far. It’ll only take about thirty minutes to bake.”

“Let’s go back to the house, then.”

She let him go ahead. “It seems nothing’s broken if you can walk so well.”

He looked down. “My legs feel fine.”

“Good, you’ll have no excuse.”

He glanced at her over his shoulder. “For what?”

“When you lose. Race you to the house.” Cherish charged ahead of him.

“Hey, not fair. You had a head start.”

Cherish kept running. A few seconds later, Malachi sprinted past her and reached the door first. He stood against it, smiling at her. She could see he was trying to stop breathing hard, to make out his run was effortless.

"How did you do that?" Cherish said between breaths.

He opened the door. "I'm faster and stronger."

She moved through, smiling to herself about the flour that was still left on his face.

CHAPTER SIXTEEN

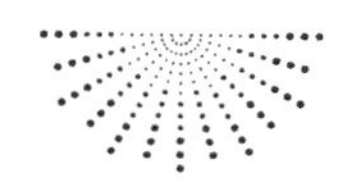

While Bliss was taking off her coat in the back room of the café, Jainie walked in. "You're about to meet the new boss."

"Hi, Jainie. I didn't know you were still working here. I heard you'd left."

Janie's lip curled. "Is that why you walked past me without looking at me?"

"No. It's because of what you did to my house."

"Jainie, get back to your station. I've got coffee orders that have just come in."

They both turned to see Marlie at the door.

Jainie hurried out without saying a word while Bliss put her coat on a hanger.

Marlie moved forward. "You must be Cherish's sister."

"I am."

"You don't look like her."

Bliss turned to face her. "I know, people say that all the time. It's because we're not really sisters. Cherish's mother married my father a couple of years ago."

"Oh, that explains it."

"Do you really think we're that different? I always thought we looked kind of similar."

"You look nothing alike. And I won't know how else the two of you are different until I see if you're a good worker or not. Do you want to stand around yapping to the customers all day, too?"

"You mean talking?"

"Yes."

"Not really. Cherish is more of a talker than I am." Bliss stood tall. "I'm determined to do a good job for you today."

Marlie tilted her head, peering at her. "I hope so. You better get out there. The place is starting to fill up."

"Yes, I will." Bliss hurried out and then grabbed a notepad and pen off the counter, ready to start taking orders.

BY THE END of Bliss's four-hour shift, she was drained and looking forward to going back to the slower pace of the orchard. She'd managed to get one person's order wrong and gave someone else the wrong change. Both errors were fixed pretty quickly, and no one had acted upset with her.

She headed into the backroom to get her things and found herself face-to-face with Marlie, again.

"You've worked hard all day. I couldn't fault you. Cherish thinks it's her job to talk to the customers. I know that's part of it, but not as much of it as she thinks.

People come here for good food and good coffee, and that's what'll keep them coming back. Cherish thinks she needs to make friends with everyone."

Bliss had to say something nice about Cherish because she wanted Marlie to think well of her step-sister. "She does her best, and she loves it here."

"Yes, I know she does. I have no doubt about that."

"I'm not going to be picked up for another hour. Is it okay if I take up a table and sit down and have a cup of coffee and something to eat?"

Marlie's face softened into a smile. "Of course you can, and don't forget your staff discount. I'll get it for you—what will you have?"

"Thanks. A caramel latte and a lemon cake, please. I can get it."

"No, I'll do it. You sit down and rest."

"Thank you."

Bliss sat down at the table next to the window. From there, she had a great view of passersby. A stooped old lady carrying two shopping bags walked slowly past. Bliss felt a little sorry for her and hoped she didn't have to go too far. Why didn't she have one of those little wheeled carts she saw old people pull behind them? She needed one of those. Then Bliss noticed two teenagers walking past, holding hands.

Bliss sighed when her mind wandered to Adam. What was he doing right now? She sat her elbows on the table and set her chin in her hands.

Was Adam thinking about her right now? He was never far from her mind. Was it the same for him?

Once she had people watched for a couple of minutes,

she headed toward the stand that held magazines for the patrons to read while they ate. But before she got there, she saw somebody had left a newspaper on one of the tables. She grabbed that instead and then sat back down. From the date, she knew it was today's newspaper.

After she'd had enough of reading about politics, she flipped over the first pages. Just as she did so, Marlie brought over her coffee and her cake.

"This is my treat, Bliss. The lemon cake's the last piece."

Bliss looked up at her. "Oh, are you sure?"

"Yes."

"Thank you so much."

Marlie headed back to the counter. Bliss was happy to have a day's pay, some money she'd gotten for tips, and now she had free cake and coffee. She'd also gotten away from the orchard and the house chores for a whole day. It felt like a dream. This is what it felt like to live Cherish's life.

Could the day get any better? Bliss wondered.

Bliss was halfway through her cake and coffee when she saw it in the newspaper.

The name had sprung out from the page and grabbed her attention.

Our Daniel Whitcombe, it read, *Victim of Violence.*

Cherish was often talking about Daniel Whitcombe. Could it be the same one?

She read on.

The news article said he was a journalist for the very paper she was reading. It had to be the same Daniel Whitcombe they knew.

Bliss left her coffee and cake and asked to use the phone. She called home and asked for Cherish's farm number, hoping there was a phone in the barn. She was positive there was.

Favor answered the phone. "No, Bliss. There's no phone in her barn, never has been."

"I need to get a message to her."

"I have the number of Ruth who lives next door to her. She'll give Cherish a message."

"Perfect. What's her number?" Bliss grabbed a pen and paper and scribbled it down.

She hung up on Favor, forgetting to even say goodbye, and immediately called Ruth. She was thankful Ruth answered immediately.

"Ruth, I am Cherish's sister, Bliss. She needs to know that something has happened. Is there any way you can get in touch with her and have her call me back?"

"Cherish is on her farm right now?"

"Yes, she's there."

"I didn't know. She hasn't come to visit me like she has every other time. Oh dear, I hope she's not upset with me about something. It could be something Malachi's said about me. Whatever he said, it's not true."

Bliss repeated, "Can you have her call me?"

"I guess I could do that. I'll go over there now. I saw Malachi's buggy go past with an aged couple in it. Thought it might've been Malachi's grandparents."

"Good, thank you. Tell her I'll be home after five. She can call me then. It's Bliss."

"Yes, I got that, Bliss."

"Thanks so much, Ruth."

"Rightio. Bye for now."

"Bye." Bliss ended the call and then sat down to a half cup of cold latte and a half-eaten piece of cake, thinking about how upset Cherish would be. Cherish had been fond of Daniel before he'd disappointed her. And Cherish wasn't the type to like many people, not the way she had liked Daniel.

Jainie sat down opposite. "Everything okay? You look panicked."

She couldn't trust Jainie with any information. "No, it's fine. I just had to tell my sister about something."

"About what?"

"Just something that I remembered that I forgot to tell her."

"If you say so, but you seem pretty upset about something."

"It's nothing much."

"I thought we were friends, Bliss."

"Yeah, we were... until you nearly burned my house down."

"That wasn't my fault. Anyway, I was drunk at the time, and I can't be held accountable for that kind of thing. That was a long time ago. Don't you ever let anything go?"

"Not much."

"Cherish and I are friends."

"That's nice."

"Suit yourself. I'll remember we're not friends." Jainie got up and walked away. Bliss then noticed Marlie had seen their interaction. It wasn't a good way to finish the day. Marlie and the bigger boss, Rocky, liked the staff to get along, but it didn't matter anyway because Cherish would be back next week.

Bliss picked up the paper and read the news article again when she heard the horse and buggy. She looked up and saw through the window that it was her father who'd come to pick her up. She put her fingers on the last two crumbs and popped them into her mouth before she took her dishes over to the counter. After a quick wave to the staff, she headed out the door.

"What kind of day did you have?" Levi asked as she climbed up into the buggy.

"Pretty good, but it's hard work."

"But you liked it, *jah?*"

"I did. I like watching everyone who comes in, and I wonder what they're doing. Are they working, do they have a day off, are they shopping? Everyone seems so busy."

"You have a busy life too, Bliss." He checked the rearview mirror and directed the horse onto the road.

"Not really. I'm not going out to a job."

"What does that matter?" Levi asked. "It doesn't mean it's not proper work."

"Cherish is allowed to work one day outside the orchard, so why can't I? It's just not fair."

"It might not be fair. There are many things in life that aren't fair. You should get used to it."

It was the answer he always gave her, which wasn't really an answer at all. It was useless. He would never allow her to work at the café, not even one day a week. "Wilma allows Cherish to work."

"She's probably glad to get her out of the *haus*. You're my daughter, so you do what I say."

"I can't figure it out. You don't want Cherish to work at the café?"

"If I had my way, she wouldn't."

"You're the head of the household, aren't you, *Dat?*"

"I am, but it's a delicate problem." He looked over at her. "Do you want me to stop Cherish from going to her job?"

"No, but I don't see why it's a, um, 'delicate problem.' I don't see why it needs to be."

"That's just the way it is."

Bliss leaned back in the buggy, feeling sick. Why couldn't she have the same privileges as Cherish since she was older?

"You can't complain about your life, Bliss. We have Adam over for dinner nearly every night."

"Yes, thank you. I am happy about that."

"You should concentrate on the good things that Wilma and I do for you."

"Okay, I'll try."

He glanced over at her. "I don't want you to ask me to let you work at the café again, ever."

She sighed and looked out the window.

CHAPTER SEVENTEEN

Later that same evening, Cherish and Malachi sat listening to Samuel and Ada talk about what they'd found during their drive in the buggy, and about their visit to the local bishop.

When they heard a car, Malachi walked over to the window. "It's Ruth, the neighbor."

Cherish's hand flew to her mouth. "Oh no! I should've visited her before now."

"She's an *Englisher?*" Ada asked.

"Yes, I told you about her. She's the nearest neighbor."

"I thought that was Rita."

"She's the closest neighbor on the other side."

Ada shook her head. "You can't have two closest neighbors."

"Will it make you happy if I pace out the distance one day?" Cherish asked.

"You don't have to be smart-mouthed about it. If you can't be accurate, you shouldn't make a statement."

"I'm sorry. I'll just see what Ruth wants." Cherish followed Malachi out the door.

"Yes, why don't you do that?" Ada called after her.

Cherish didn't like apologizing when she didn't believe she'd done anything wrong, but sometimes it was easier to say sorry when she didn't mean it rather than have a lengthy conversation about something. Malachi and Cherish got to the car just as Ruth was getting out.

"Hi, Ruth. New car?" Cherish asked as Malachi walked a full circle around it.

"Yes, I traded in the pickup truck. I figured I'd spoil myself."

"Why not? It's nice," Malachi said.

"I shouldn't have bothered getting a new car, though, for going over all these dusty roads. I can never keep it clean."

Cherish had noticed the bright red car had a layer of dust and some mud splashes in the lower section. "I can see that it would be hard to keep clean. You should come in and meet my mother's best friend. She and her husband came with me."

"Yes, I'll do that in a minute, but your sister called me in a dreadful panic."

Cherish's fingertips flew to her throat. "Is Caramel alright?"

"Who?"

"It's Cherish's dog," Malachi told her.

Ruth pursed her lips at Malachi and then turned back to Cherish. "I don't know. She wouldn't tell me what the problem was. She wants you to call her back. You can use my phone." Ruth stuck her head in the car window and handed over her cell phone. "Said she'd be home after five."

"What's the time now?"

Ruth looked at her wristwatch. "A little before five."

"I'll call her now."

"You know how to use it?" asked Ruth.

"Yes. I've used them before."

With another disapproving glance at Malachi, Ruth said, "I'll sit in the car until you've finished."

Malachi shrugged his shoulders. "Then I guess I'll wait right here and talk to myself."

It was a tense moment. Ruth didn't like Malachi, and she didn't mind showing it, but Cherish had bigger things to worry about. As she walked a few steps away, she dialed her home number.

Bliss answered.

"Bliss, it's Cherish, what is it?"

"I went to work today to take over from you."

"Oh no, they didn't fire you, did they, or did they fire me? Oh no, what's happening?"

"No one got fired. My shift finished at three, but no one could pick me up until four, so I was waiting in the café drinking a caramel latte and eating a piece of cake, and I was reading the paper someone had left."

"What, Bliss? Just spit it out."

"I just started reading it, and you know what I found?"

"No, just tell me."

"Daniel Whitcombe is in the hospital. The paper said people set upon him with a baseball bat and now he's in the hospital with a broken leg and a concussion."

"Are you serious? Is it the same Daniel?"

"I'm serious, and yes, it's the same Daniel."

"Did it say Whitcombe or Withers?"

"Whitcombe."

Cherish looked back at Malachi, who was watching her, standing next to the car.

She looked away. Could Malachi have sent some people to do this to Daniel?

He said he'd fix things.

Was this his way of doing that?

If it wasn't him, it sure was a coincidence.

"Cherish, are you there?"

"I'm here. I'm just in shock."

"I thought you'd want to know. I know you hate him now, but you once liked him."

"I don't hate him. I just don't like him anymore because he hasn't got good morals. Thanks for letting me know. Is everything else okay at home? What about Caramel?"

"Caramel's fine."

"Is he missing me, a little?"

"Maybe a little bit, but everyone's paying him lots of attention, and he's loving it. He's still sleeping on your bed every night."

"Oh, he's missing me. I know it."

"If you say so. Anyway, I better go and help with the dinner. At least I'll offer. I'm hoping they'll tell me not to because I've been at the café all day." Bliss giggled. "I'm living your life for a day, and I'm loving it."

Cherish wasn't listening. "Thanks for letting me know about Daniel." Cherish pressed end and then walked back to give Ruth the phone.

"Men problems?" Ruth asked as she got out of the car. "I didn't mean to listen, but I heard the name Daniel. Is he your beau?" Ruth's eyes twinkled with delight.

"No. He's someone we know who got attacked, and he's in the hospital."

"One of your Amish people?"

"No, a reporter who was threatening to do some stories, and I asked him not to. We had quite an argument. Several of them."

"Oh, that's too bad. I hope the police aren't going to knock on your door about it."

"Knock on my door? Why would they?"

Ruth grimaced. "If you had a fight or disagreement with him and next thing he ends up attacked, they're going to put two and two together. They'll want to talk with you at least. I watch all the detective shows on TV, Perry Mason, The Saint, and Hawaii Five-O."

Cherish swallowed hard. Would Daniel tell the police Cherish was his enemy? "No, it wasn't like that."

"You better introduce me to your friends. I saw them driving past my house in Malachi's buggy."

"Yes, sure, c'mon in the house." Cherish took her inside, and Malachi followed.

CHAPTER EIGHTEEN

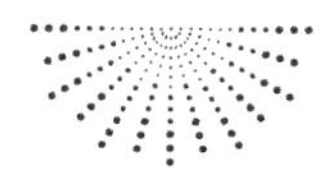

After Cherish made the introductions, Ada and Ruth immediately began talking between themselves while Samuel tried to involve himself by commenting here and there on what they'd said.

With both Samuel and Ada distracted by Ruth, Cherish pulled Malachi into the kitchen by his sleeve.

He frowned at her once they were alone. "What are you doing?"

"Bliss had an urgent message for me. The reporter I told you about is in the hospital, barely alive. People attacked him and left him lying in an alley." She wasn't sure if the part about the alley was correct, but that's how she imagined it.

"That's dreadful. Is that what you were talking about on the phone? I didn't want to ask."

"Yes." She stared into his eyes. "Tell me something, truthfully."

"What?"

"Did you have anything to do with the attack on him?"

His jaw dropped. "Why would you say that? I'd never hurt anyone, and anyway, I've been here the whole time."

"You said you'd do something about him and you seemed pretty confident you could stop him. Is this the way you did it? Did you send someone to threaten him?"

"Of course not."

Cherish wasn't convinced. He didn't seem outraged by her accusation. "You seemed pretty confident you could stop him," she repeated.

"What kind of a person do you think I am, Cherish Baker? I meant I would pray for you and for the whole situation to be resolved."

She lowered her head, ashamed of herself for suspecting him when he meant he'd pray. That's why he was so confident. He had faith in *Gott*. She felt awful.

"You don't know me at all, Cherish."

She got an instant headache. "I'm so sorry. It's just that I've been around some horrible people, and I'm not used to being around nice people. It seems everyone lets me down, and I thought…"

"You thought what? I was just another creep who'd let you down?"

She could barely talk because of the lump in her throat. "Yes."

"Well, I'm not, and I'm not a criminal either. I'd never do anything like that."

With a big swallow of air, she said, "I'm sorry, I don't know what I was thinking."

"Best we go out there and talk to the others." He walked ahead of her, shaking his head.

No sooner did Ruth leave than Annie arrived.

Malachi had looked out the window and spotted her once they were all back inside after waving goodbye to Ruth. "It's Annie."

Cherish moved next to him and looked out the window. "Were you expecting her?"

"I don't think so."

"What's she doing here?"

He shrugged his shoulders. "Let's go and find out." He hurried out the door.

"You say it's Annie here again?" asked Ada.

"That's right."

"*Wunderbaar.*"

Cherish headed off to catch up with Malachi.

"Nice to see you again," Cherish heard Malachi say. The way he spoke wasn't like they were girlfriend and boyfriend. It wasn't the softly spoken way Fairfax would speak to Hope or how Adam would talk to Bliss.

"I have brought something over for Ada and Samuel to take home. It's a gingerbread house."

"Hi again, Annie," Cherish said. "A gingerbread house, she'll love that. She'll probably show all her friends and say she made it." Cherish laughed.

Annie didn't even smile. "I don't think she'd do that."

"No, I didn't really mean it. It was a joke."

"Cherish likes to joke and be funny," Malachi explained.

Cherish frowned. That's not how she would've described herself. She never joked, well, hardly ever. "My older sister's husband, Stephen, is the joker of the family. Samuel likes to laugh at jokes, but he can never remember any of them to share. He wrote some down to tell me once, but they're not as funny when they're read out."

Annie remained silent and opened the back of the buggy. Malachi pulled out a box, and Annie helped him steady it until it was safely in his arms.

"Okay, I've got it," he said.

Both girls walked into the house behind Malachi. It was so close to dinner that they would have to ask Annie if she wanted to stay. This was probably Annie's secret plan all along.

As soon as he walked in the door, Malachi turned around to face them. "I'll put this on the kitchen table then, shall I?"

"I guess so," said Annie.

"Hello, Annie, I didn't know we'd be seeing you again today."

Annie's face lit up, and she hurried over to sit down with Ada. "I brought you a surprise, Ada. My mother made a special gingerbread house for you to take home with you. She said it would be easier to have one in front of you while you're making another."

Ada clapped her hands together, and then she hugged Annie. "Thank you. You must thank your mother for me. That's wonderful. I can't wait to try it. That will be my new specialty."

"What's your old specialty?" Annie asked.

Samuel said, "She has many specialties. Everything she cooks is wonderful."

"Her chocolate chip cookies are the best," Cherish said.

Ada's face beamed with delight.

"It's a shame you're not staying longer then, so you would've been able to give me some cooking tips."

Ada gave a little shrug. "I don't really have any. I'm sure your mother is a good cook too."

"She's better with sweets and desserts, candies and such. "

Cherish felt she should be the one to say it because she knew someone would. "Annie, would you like to stay for dinner for the evening meal?"

"Oh, I couldn't impose like that."

"I guess your mother is expecting you back. Maybe another time, then."

"No, she's not expecting me. If I don't come back, she'll know I'm here."

"Please stay," said Ada. "I've got so much to talk about. We have so much in common."

Cherish said, "But if you didn't tell your mother you're coming here for dinner, she'll set a meal out for you."

"That will be fine. We always make more than we need anyway. We use them as leftovers."

"Great, so you're staying then?" Cherish smiled, although on the inside, she was dreading Annie dominating the conversation again. This was her stay at the farm. This trip was supposed to be about her, not about Annie and her gingerbread houses.

"Okay, I will stay. How can I say no when everyone wants me to stay longer?"

"*Wunderbaar.*" Cherish walked to the kitchen to get away from everyone.

CHAPTER NINETEEN

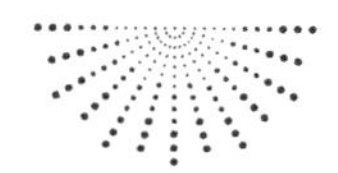

That night Cherish stayed up late and washed the dishes with Malachi.

"You were quiet over dinner. Why was that?" Cherish dug him in the ribs with her elbow.

"Ow, that hurt."

"Tell me the truth. Why have you been so quiet? Don't you like us being here? We'll be gone soon, so don't worry."

He shook his head. "It's not that."

"Tell me, then."

"I couldn't get a word in between Annie and Ada. And, I know nothing much about cooking so I couldn't join in the conversation. I only know how to boil a few potatoes and fry a slab of meat. What do I know about making figures out of hard sugar frosting?"

"Well you might have learned something tonight."

"Yeah, but is it anything I'll ever need to know?" He shook his head again.

"What would you rather have talked about?"

"Anything else would've been better. I could've talked to Samuel about farming."

"You still can."

"No, they've gone to bed now. I can only talk to you."

Cherish shrugged. "I'm sorry for it only being me."

He laughed as he handed her another plate to dry. "Don't be sorry. I like talking to you."

"I know, that's what you say in all your letters, so I've come to believe it."

"Good, you should believe everything I say."

"Yeah, but writing that all the time in your letters made me think something else."

"Like what?" He turned to look at her, and she saw that water was dripping from his hands onto the floor.

She grabbed them and directed them back over the sink. "I've only just swept the floor. I don't want to wash it as well."

"Tell me about what you just said. What idea did you get?" he asked.

"I thought you liked me, had a crush on me, or something stupid."

"No way! I'll have to be more careful with what I say. I can't have you thinking I like you." He grinned as he turned his attention back to the dishes.

"I know. How do you think I felt? First Eddie tells me he likes me and then if you did, I might get a big head." She put another dry plate beside her with the others. "You wouldn't want Annie to think there was something between us. She would be jealous."

"I doubt it very much."

"Oh, so you don't think she'd see me as a threat to her relationship with you?"

"Not at all."

"That's so rude and hurtful." She made a face.

"Depends on how you look at it."

"What way did you mean it?"

"I've got nothin' going on with Annie."

"Yeah, well, I'm not convinced about that. One minute you're not, one minute you are. I can't figure it out."

"There's nothing to figure out. We're friends."

"It seems a bit weird to me that you have a girl that's a friend. Where I come from, men have men friends."

"Yeah, ever heard that saying about beggars can't be choosers? There are not too many people I can be friends with around here, is there? Since I'm working on your farm, maybe it's your fault I have no men friends."

"If I had my farm in a more populated area, I'd probably have a different farm manager."

"Ouch, that hurt. You know how to kick a guy when he's down."

Cherish realized what she had said. "I'm sorry. I didn't mean that. You're doing a good job, you are."

He laughed. "I think I am."

"You are. Don't worry about me. Sometimes I don't think enough before I say things, and then they come out wrong anyway."

"I know. I've come to learn that about you." He pulled out the plug, and the water drained away and then he shook his hands in the sink and went to wipe them on his clothes.

"Ach! Malachi, don't do that?" She passed him a hand

towel. "You have to take care of your clothes and then you won't have to wash them as often."

"I wash once a week. My clothes that is."

Her eyebrows rose. "Good to know."

He put away her large stack of dry dishes.

"What will we do now? Are we going to sit up and talk or what?" Cherish asked.

"Yeah, if you want."

"What would you normally do on a normal day if we weren't here?"

"Well, I'll probably be doing some repairs on something."

"Like what?"

"Sewing patches over the holes in the burlap sacks or sewing up holes in my clothes or repairing the leather-work that we use on the harnesses. Whittling wood is another thing I like to do."

Cherish couldn't think of anything more boring, and her face must've said as much.

"What would you do?" he asked.

"After dinner at home, we all used to sit around and have a Bible reading and Levi would lead it, but we don't do that so much anymore, not since his heart attack. I'm not sure why. He often reads the Bible by himself while *Mamm* sews or knits."

"That sounds like a peaceful life."

"I guess. She's making baby clothes now for my two sisters who are having babies in Connecticut. Both sisters are having their second babies around the same time as each other, and when they had their first babies they had them… Wait, I have to think. They even had them on the same day or a day apart. That's bad. I should write all these things down to remember them."

"Memory loss at your age." He made tsk tsk sounds and shook his head.

"That's not real memory loss. It's just that I have to have so many things to remember my brain can only hold so much. I'm getting so many nieces and nephews I'll have to write down their birthdays. I've got two nieces and two nephews. And two more are coming. What do you think the next two will be, boys or girls?"

He closed the cupboard door after putting the dishes away. "One of each, I'd say, to keep it even."

"I think it will be two more girls. Girls are so much nicer."

"Hey, I thought you were done insulting me."

"You're not a boy. You're a man."

"Thanks for noticing."

Cherish slid into a kitchen chair and stared at the gingerbread house. "What's the big deal?" She poked at the frosting on the roof.

"Don't break it, whatever you do. Ada will never forgive you."

"I just want to smash it."

He sat opposite. "Are you serious right now? Why are you so angry?"

Her eyes met his. "I'm not angry."

"Smashing something is aggressive."

"I'm not. It's kind of like when you're walking past people eating ice creams. You get an urge to push it in their faces."

He laughed, leaning away from her.

"Ever feel like that?" she asked.

"No, I've never considered it."

"Do it, next time you see someone eating an ice cream."

"Thanks to you, I won't be able to *not* think about it."

"Do it now. Close your eyes and picture it."

He frowned.

"Go on," she ordered.

He closed his eyes.

"Now you're walking down the street, and there are two children eating ice creams, and they're walking toward you."

"Children? That's mean. I can't do it."

"You're no fun. Okay, the children turn around and walk away from you, and two adults walk up eating ice cream."

"That's better."

"Okay, so these two adults are getting closer, and they're enjoying their ice creams so much. They're holding them so close to their faces. It wouldn't take much to push it into their faces. Then you just run away. Do it now."

He kept his eyes closed, and then he smiled before he opened them "Please tell me you've never done that, Cherish."

"No. Just thought about it."

He sighed. "Now that's all I'll think about when I see someone eating an ice cream."

She looked down at the gingerbread house. "I guess it is pretty cute. And I can see why Ada is so excited to be making them."

He crossed his arms and sat his elbows on the table. "And what things do you get excited about, Cherish Baker?"

"Moving to the farm when I'm older. That's all I'm living for."

"I don't like to hear that. That means I'll have to move out."

"I can't help that. You knew it from the start."

"Yeah, but I kind of got attached to this place." He looked around the kitchen. "I'll have to un-attach myself."

She couldn't help noticing how long and perfect his eyelashes were. Eyelashes like those were wasted on a man. When he looked and caught her staring, she looked away. "I'll give you plenty of notice."

"Thanks, I guess."

"Don't worry. It won't be for a long time. You might be ready to move away from here before then."

"Doubt it."

"Don't make me feel bad."

"Sorry. I didn't mean to," he said, still staring at her.

When she stared back at him, he didn't look away as she thought he would. She enjoyed his company more than she ever had, which was one reason she didn't want to go home. She'd miss him and his tousled hair, his stubbly chin that needed a closer shave, and those eyelashes. She sprang to her feet. "I'll see you in the morning."

He leaned back. "Aren't you going to stay up and talk?"

"I'm tired, and we've already talked."

"Aw, Cherish."

She hurried out of the room. When she got changed

and slipped under the quilt, she ran through all the reasons that a man like Malachi was a bad match.

He was untidy, he didn't listen to any of her advice, and he had that unreasonable fear of chickens.

And finally, she'd never be able to boss him about like Ada did to Samuel. That last reason caused Cherish to laugh into her pillow.

CHAPTER TWENTY

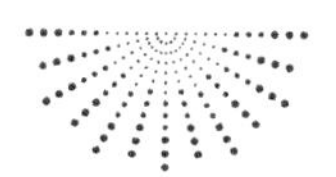

Cherish blinked back tears as they drove away from the farm. She looked out the back window and saw Malachi still waving, getting smaller and smaller. Now it was back to the mundane life on the orchard where everyone told her what to do.

It wasn't long before Samuel's head rolled to the side, and he started snoring, thankfully, much more quietly than he snored at night.

"How did you like your stay?" Ada asked.

"I loved it. Thanks again for coming with me."

"You're welcome. I'm so pleased I got to meet Annie and her mother. They're such lovely people."

Cherish wasn't so sure about Annie. "I think you can't wait to get home to make your own gingerbread house."

"That's right. I'm going to start on one as soon as I can."

"That's nice." Cherish stared out the window. Maybe Samuel had the right idea about sleeping through the long journey, but she couldn't because Ada kept talking.

"It's a shame that Hope is planning to marry Fairfax because I saw her with a different man."

Cherish faced her. "Who?"

"Jonathon and Stephen's younger brother."

An image of their annoying brother popped into her mind. "Matthew?"

"That's right."

"He's younger than she is."

"Only by a year, that's not much at all. I'm three years older than Samuel."

Cherish gasped. "That's something I didn't know. You're older than your husband, and you were complaining about Miriam being older than Earl?"

Ada scoffed. "It's hardly the same. We're talking three years, which is nothing. And we had children. We were so young when we met."

Cherish laughed. "They'd call you a cradle snatcher for being older. No wait, there's another name, a lioness. No, that's not right. It's a cougar."

Ada's mouth turned down at the corners. "I hardly think that's an appropriate thing to say."

"Sorry."

"We had *kinner.* I don't think that your half-brother will ever have any. And I don't know what's going on with Christina." Ada pressed her mouth together, disapprovingly.

"She wants children, but she just hasn't been able to have them, that's all. I wonder if she should go see a doctor."

"She probably has already done that by now. They've been married for years."

Cherish bit her lip. "If Mark doesn't have children and Earl doesn't, then it would be so sad for them."

"See, that's what your *mudder* and I were concerned about. We were only thinking about Earl. He took it that we didn't like Miriam, but we did."

"I understand now you say it like that, but they are in love, so I don't think they care about that. They can always adopt."

Ada rolled her eyes. "That's what people always say, but it's not that easy."

"They might come across a woman who doesn't want to keep her baby."

"That doesn't happen often."

"But maybe—"

"Enough, Cherish. Just be realistic. That's all I'm saying. That's the best advice I can give you if you choose to take it. You probably won't. You're way too stubborn. My matchmaking gift worked out for Mercy and Honor."

"I think Mercy was ready to marry anybody. She doesn't even understand her husband's jokes."

"That doesn't mean they weren't meant for each other. I saw that they were, and that's why I knew they'd be good together. There are Honor and Jonathon, too."

"They do seem suited. I mean, the others do as well. I'm not saying they're not well matched. Just between you and me, Matthew is annoying."

"I think you'll be surprised. He might have grown into a very handsome man since you last saw him."

"Yeah, 'Handsome is as handsome does, I've heard that said. Even if he is the most beautiful man in the world, it's his personality that'll be his downfall."

"People change, and you don't have to be rude."

Cherish's mouth fell open. "Ada, you know I'm not a rude person. *Mamm* raised me as well as can be. The problem with him last time was he liked Hope and he wouldn't stop hanging around her."

"That's too bad. You see what I say? Matthew liked Hope, and now she's promised to Fairfax who isn't one of us, not really."

"Fairfax is one of us now, officially, and in the sight of *Gott.*" Ada was the mean one.

"I know he is in a way, but the ones who aren't born into the faith are the first ones to leave at the first sign of a struggle."

Cherish looked out the window again, wishing she was back at the farm.

Ada wasn't stopping there. "Too many people think *Gott* is a gift giver. Say your prayers and you can have what you want, but it doesn't work like that. Once these people find out their life isn't going to be perfect, they leave us."

Cherish kept staring at the trees swishing by. "No, it doesn't."

"Doesn't what?"

"Whatever you said."

"That's why he'd be a better man for Hope."

"Jah, he would," Cherish said, hoping Ada would be quiet.

"I think it's time for young Matthew to come for a visit."

"Why not wait for harvest time?" Cherish suggested, thinking his annoyingness would be swallowed up in the usual harvest crowd that came to the orchard.

"I think we need to do it sooner."

Cherish looked back out the window. If she tried to talk Ada out of it, that would only spur her on.

CHAPTER TWENTY-ONE

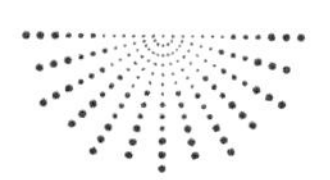

It was dark when the car pulled up at the Baker/Bruner household. Cherish was home, and she was glad to be there. Also, spending all that time in a confined space with Ada had been draining. Relief had come with a couple of car problems where they were all able to get out of the vehicle to stretch their legs.

"Here we are," Ada said, meaning they were finally home.

"Here I am," Cherish corrected her.

Ada laughed. "Yes. Samuel and I will be home in a few minutes. Tell Wilma I'll stop by tomorrow and see how she is."

"And to catch up on all the gossip." Cherish opened the car door while the driver opened the trunk.

"It's not gossip, Cherish, it's news."

"Okay. Thanks for taking me up there. I appreciate it. You too, Samuel."

Samuel raised a hand. "You're welcome."

"I'd like to say we'd do it again, but we're so booked

up with going hither and thither, I don't know when we'll be able to take you. But we enjoyed it."

"I'm glad. I'll see you tomorrow." Cherish closed the door and joined the driver at the back of the car.

"This yours, miss?" He held up her bag.

"That's the one. Thanks."

Cherish took hold of the bag and walked up to the house, hearing the car that was leaving. It was a little odd that no one had come out to meet her. Surely they'd heard them arrive.

She walked in and put her bag down before she shut the door behind her. The first thing she wanted to do was check on Timmy, but she didn't want to disturb his sleep.

Levi was on the couch asleep. She had a closer look at him. What if he wasn't sleeping? He was so still; he looked like he could be dead. Usually, his beard moved up and down with every breath when he was resting.

Memories of his heart attack came flooding back. The doctor hadn't given him any guarantees.

In the quietness of the night, she studied him, hoping he wasn't dead. She'd grown a tiny bit fond of him over the years. She crept closer and closer, looking for some kind of movement, some sign.

Then, she had the idea to put her hand under his nose to see if she could feel his breath on her hand.

Swallowing hard, she got closer and closer and then put her hand up to his face.

He snorted a large snore that sent Cherish jumping back about six feet, and she knocked over the small table where Levi kept his Bible. Something broke and the remnants skidded across the floor.

Levi opened his eyes. "Cherish? What are you doing on the floor?"

She looked around. "Um... I just knocked over the table and broke the coffee mug. I'm sorry."

He smiled. "We've got more. It doesn't matter. When did you get home?"

"Just a few minutes ago. Where is everyone?"

"Asleep, I'd say."

"Why aren't you in bed?"

"Someone had to wait up for you."

"Thank you. That's nice. Do you want me to get you anything?"

"Nee denke." He rose to his feet. "It's time for me to go up to bed. We'll talk about your visit to the farm in the morning. We're all waiting to hear your news."

Cherish picked herself up off the floor. "I've got plenty to tell. Ada's coming tomorrow too, and she can tell you her news."

"Wunderbaar. Night, Cherish. Welcome home."

"Denke. Gut nacht, Levi."

Cherish cleaned up the mess she'd made and then headed upstairs to bed, forgetting all about the bag she'd left by the door.

When she got to her room, she found Caramel on her bed. He opened his eyes sleepily, then gave a quiet 'woof' and wagged his tail.

"I've missed you so much, Caramel."

She gave him lots of hugs and then slipped between the covers. After the long day she'd had, a bed had never felt so good.

CHAPTER TWENTY-TWO

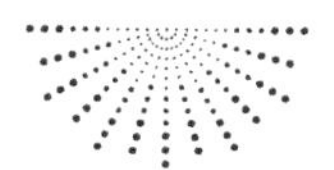

When light streamed into Cherish's bedroom the next morning, she covered her face with a pillow, hoping for a little more sleep.

"Are you awake, Cherish?"

Cherish pulled off the pillow to see Favor. "I am now."

"Sorry." She sat on the bed. "So how was it? Are you happy with how he was keeping the farm?"

Cherish pushed herself up onto her elbows. "I am. I think he's doing a good job. I've got to come up with a few hundred dollars somehow because the barn needs repairing."

"Where are we going to find that kind of money?"

"I'm not sure yet."

Mamm stuck her head around the edge of the doorway. "Don't look at me."

"I wasn't going to ask you or Levi. I don't want to be in debt to anybody."

"What does Malachi say about it?" *Mamm* asked.

"I told him to sell something and he said there's nothing to sell."

"This is what happens when you have a farm with no money to run it. There'll be expenses. Most people have a bank overdraft in situations like this."

"That's a brilliant idea, the bank."

Mamm shook her head. "No, Cherish, because then you'll have to pay it back."

"I can pay it off over time."

"Won't the men in the community help to repair the barn?"

"Of course they will—this is just the amount for the wood to fix it. The men will help rebuild it and paint it and all that for nothing."

"Must be some kind of extensive repair."

"It is. It's half the back of the barn. And you know how large the barn is."

"I do."

"Malachi asked about you."

"He did?" *Mamm's* face simply glowed with delight.

"Yes, he did."

"How nice of him. I'll make a start on breakfast," *Mamm* said.

"I'll help." Favor followed *Mamm* out of her room.

"We should get ready too, Caramel." Cherish looked down to see she'd forgotten to change out of the clothes she was wearing yesterday. She got out of bed and looked down at her clothes. They seemed clean. She'd change after she had a shower later today, but right now, all she could think about was food. She headed downstairs to join the others.

As soon as she was seated at the table, Levi walked into the kitchen. "You arrived late, Cherish."

"It was car problems. First, there was a flat tire, and once we got on the road again, we stopped to get gas, and then the car wouldn't start. It had a low battery."

"That's unbelievable," *Mamm* commented.

"I know, but at least I'm here now. Ada said she'd talk to you today. She was weary. Now I've got you both here, I have a favor to ask."

"And what is this about?" Levi sat down.

"If I could, I would just like one more day off."

Levi narrowed his eyes. "You're meant to go to the coffee shop today."

"I know, but they won't mind if Bliss goes there instead of me."

Wilma and Levi looked at one another.

Mamm said, "She did arrive home very late. And she would be fatigued from the trip."

He frowned. "So you want to have a rest? Is that it?"

"Not really. What I want to do is visit a friend who is in the hospital. I could drive Bliss to the café and then go to the hospital from there."

"Who is this friend?"

"It's the reporter who did the story on our apple orchard sometime back."

Levi rubbed his beard. "I didn't know you knew him that well."

"I do. I bumped into him a few times in town, and we've talked."

"I'm very pleased you have the compassion to visit somebody who is in the hospital, Cherish."

"Thanks, *Mamm.*"

"Jah, I suppose that's all right. As long as it's all right with Bliss and your employer, I'll allow it."

"Denke, Levi and *Mamm.* Did anything happen here while I was gone?"

"Nothing out of the ordinary. We had no visitors with Ada gone. We didn't even see Joy or anyone. It was a strange week."

"You better see if Bliss wants to take your place again. She'll need to wake soon so she won't be late."

Cherish sprang to her feet. "I'll wake her." Cherish ran up the stairs and burst into Bliss's room to see her fully dressed and about to place her prayer *kapp* on her head.

"You're home." Bliss dropped the *kapp* on her bed, ran to Cherish, and hugged her.

Cherish patted Bliss on her back, and then the girls parted. "I have a surprise."

"For me?"

"Jah. How would you like to work at the café again today?"

"I'd love it. The only thing is, Jainie and I had a few words."

"About what?"

"About how she burned down our house, nearly."

Cherish swiped a hand through the air. "That was a long time ago, and she had too much to drink."

Bliss pursed her lips. "That's what she said, but still…"

"Ah, don't worry about it. Just let it go, do your job, and let her do hers."

Bliss sighed. "Okay. I'm excited to have another day there. How come you don't want to go?"

"I'm visiting Daniel in the hospital."

"Oh. I see. Did *Dat* say I could go today?"

"*Jah,* of course, it's all been arranged."

"*Denke,* Cherish."

"No problem. I'm driving you there and picking you up."

Bliss clapped her hands together. "I can't wait."

"Let's eat, and then we'll go."

"Okay."

CHAPTER TWENTY-THREE

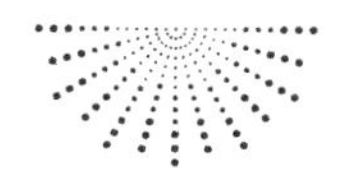

Later that day, after Cherish had taken Bliss to the café, she arrived at the hospital. She found out which room Daniel was in, got directions, and headed up in the elevator.

She followed the signs until she found his room, and peeped around the door frame. He was by himself in the room, and his eyes were closed. It was an awful sight, seeing him hooked up to machines and his leg elevated, encased in plaster. When she walked in, he opened his eyes.

"Cherish."

"Yeah, it's me. I'm sorry. I didn't mean to wake you." She moved to the edge of his bed. "What happened to you?"

"Must've upset someone."

She swallowed hard. "What do you mean?"

"Seems there were a couple of people who didn't want me to write a certain something, something."

"What is the 'something, something?'"

"I can't tell you, obviously, can I? Or next time they'll kill me. Why are you here? Did you come here because you care about me and my well-being or just come here to tell me what to write and what not to write?" His voice rose, "I'm over censorship and being held back."

Cherish was taken aback by his outburst. "I was worried about you, of course, I was, soon as I heard. I was away, otherwise, I would've come sooner."

"Away where?"

"At my farm—do you want to write about that, too?"

"No, doesn't sound interesting enough."

She moved around to the other side of the bed and sat down in the chair. "That didn't stop you before. Just make up some lies."

"No, I can't. There's no inspiration about you and your silly farm."

Cherish pulled the chair closer to the bed. "There's no need to be rude about it."

"Are you trying to make me feel better or worse?"

"I'm sorry, I'm just..."

"I don't want to listen to your problems, so go away if that's all you're going to talk about."

This was a far different Daniel. Someone *had* hit him on the head, she remembered. "I'm sorry, but I am concerned about what you'll write about my family."

"I've never met a more selfish, self-obsessed person than you."

"I'm not." Even as she spoke, she wondered if what he said was true. He wasn't the first person to say something like that. Florence often said she only thought about herself, only cared about herself, but that wasn't right.

No, it wasn't true, she told herself. She was there because this man was a threat to her family's peace of mind. "Don't make out that I'm the one in the wrong. I know you don't feel well at the moment, but you're the one threatening to ruin my family's life to make yourself look good and further your stupid career." She regretted adding that last bit, but it was too late to take it back.

"Your problem is not my problem. I don't create the stories. I just write about them."

"Yeah, whether they're true or not," Cherish snapped.

"Truth is a social construction."

Cherish had no idea what he meant. "So you're not going to write about my family, or you are?"

"Just get out!"

Cherish stood up and then looked back at him. "I feel sorry for you."

"Don't. Just go."

"Before I go, I've got some advice."

"I don't need any."

"When you're walking on a path, and you keep coming up against closed doors, maybe someone's telling you you're on the wrong path. When you're on the right path, doors open to you."

"I don't need some Sunday school saying from someone with the brain of a five-year-old."

Cherish felt her mouth drop open in shock. She was trying to be kind to him. "I'm giving you some good advice."

"I don't need advice from an Amish farm girl. Just get out of here."

"I just want to say one more thing."

He reached for his buzzer and couldn't get it. "Nurse!" he bellowed.

"Write your story, Daniel, if it means so much to you. My family will survive because we have love and compassion. We'll heal from any hurts you cause. I worry about what will happen to you after you write the story because of you being on the wrong path, and all."

"Shut up about paths!"

At that moment, a nurse walked in. "Yes? What do you need?"

"She won't leave," Daniel snapped. "I've asked her to leave, and she won't go."

The nurse looked at her and shrugged as if to say, it's his room.

"I'm going." Cherish walked out, wondering how she could've ever have liked Daniel Whitcombe or was it Withers? He wasn't a nice person. He had seemed so at one time, but he had changed.

She turned around and saw the nurse standing in the doorway with her arms folded. The woman rolled her eyes, her body language telling Cherish that Daniel was a jerk to the staff, too.

Cherish couldn't go back to make amends or say she was sorry for anything she had said—not that she regretted it—so she continued to the elevator.

Now Cherish was satisfied that she'd done all she could.

It was time to stop worrying once and for all.

CHAPTER TWENTY-FOUR

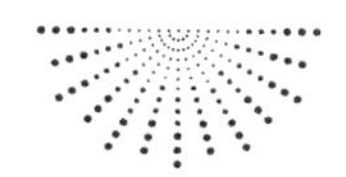

When Cherish arrived home, *Mamm* was waiting for her and demanded to be taken to Joy's. Levi had another horse and buggy ready for Cherish to drive, and he was waiting to take care of the horse she'd been driving.

Cherish was then told she was to wait in the buggy at Joy and Isaac's because *Mamm* wanted to speak to Joy privately.

Just as they pulled onto the road from the driveway, *Mamm* said, "I think there's something wrong with Joy."

"Maybe she's having another baby. Wouldn't that be great?"

"*Jah,* but it might not be that."

"Did Ada come yet?"

"*Nee,* she'll most likely come in the afternoon."

"Tell me, why are you worried about Joy?"

"I've hardly seen her."

Mamm always had to have something to fret over.

Cherish tried to make her mother feel better. "It's just that she's tired from having the baby."

"Nonsense. She'd be over that by now. It only takes a day or two to get over."

"When you had your first, wasn't Florence there to help?"

"Ach, Florence was only a young girl at the time."

"Even an eight-year-old can be of help especially if it's someone so capable as Florence. She would've been a good help at three. She could've fetched things for you and stuff like that."

"I did it all myself."

"So, what do you think is wrong with Joy?" Cherish asked again.

"I think that Christina or maybe Earl has turned her against me."

"Hmm. What if she's worried about moving out of the house?"

Mamm stared at Cherish. "She's not moving."

"But Levi said he's allowing them to stay there after they did the repairs. He didn't say they could stay there forever. Perhaps they're..."

Mamm pursed her lips. "It's about time they bought their own place. Levi's kind offer would've allowed them to save a tremendous amount. Before they lived there, they had some savings. They have never had to pay a cent in rent after they married."

"Maybe Levi has asked them to leave already."

Mamm's head whipped around to stare at Cherish. "Do you think so?"

"Could be. Has he said anything to you?"

Mamm shrugged her shoulders. "He doesn't always tell me about things. He could've talked to them. I'll ask Joy if he has."

"Don't. It'll only give her something else to worry about if it's not that."

"Now you've put that into my head, I'll have to find out."

Cherish shrugged her shoulders. "Okay. I think she's just tired. Maybe she's not getting enough sleep."

"You'll find out when you're a mother that you just know when something's wrong with one of your *kinner.* Something's off."

"Okay. I'll take your word for it." Cherish turned the horse and buggy onto Isaac and Joy's driveway. "Here we are." She stopped the buggy close to the house.

"Thank you, Cherish. I'll be as quick as I can." Wilma stepped down from the buggy.

"Don't rush. Take your time." Cherish watched her mother walk to Joy's house. Then *Mamm* stopped, turned around, and headed back to the buggy. "Have you changed your mind, *Mamm?"*

"Nee. I've just come back to tell you to stay in the buggy." She shook her finger at Cherish. "I don't want you sneaking up to the house and hiding under a window to listen in."

Cherish's mouth fell open. *"Mamm,* I would never do something awful like that. It's so wrong to eavesdrop."

Mamm narrowed her eyes, turned back around, retraced her steps toward the house, and knocked on Joy's door.

Cherish leaned back in the seat. What was she going

to do now? It was going to be so dull sitting in the buggy doing nothing. There was no telling how long they were going to be talking.

Joy opened the door to her mother. "*Mamm,* what are you doing here?"

"I've come to visit my daughter and my granddaughter."

"Oh, that's lovely of you to visit us."

Mamm pursed her lips. "You say that as though I hardly ever come here."

"That's right."

"That's not true, Joy."

"No?"

Goldie jumped up on Wilma just as she sat down on the couch.

"No, stop it, Goldie. You'll go outside," Joy warned her dog.

"Just put the dog outside, Joy. It can't be healthy having the creature around the baby."

Joy rolled her eyes and opened the door. "Out you go, Goldie."

The dog hung his head, put his tail down, and slowly headed outside.

"That's better," *Mamm* said when Joy closed the door. "Where is Faith?"

"She's asleep. I've only just put her down. If I'd known you were coming, I would've kept her awake."

Wilma placed her hands in her lap. "I've just come here to see what's wrong with you."

"What do you mean? Nothing is wrong with me."

"You can't fool me. I know something is bothering

you. You're not coming over as much as you used to."

"That's because I have a baby, and it's not so easy. I have to pack so much stuff to take her anywhere."

"It's not that. It's a different reason. I can tell." Wilma stared at her.

"Okay, you know what's really bothering me?"

"Jah," Wilma said. "If I knew, I wouldn't have had to come over here and ask."

"I feel invisible. No one cares about me. It's all about Florence and if the attention's not on her, it's on Cherish. They get the attention, they always have."

"That's not so."

"I don't think you cared as much about Faith as you did about Mercy and Honor's babies when they were born. It'll be the same when she's one, her birthday will come and go without a fuss."

"She's one already?" *Mamm* asked.

"Of course she's not. You're not even listening to me. I don't even know why you bothered coming here."

"I'm so sorry you feel that way. I've got a lot of things going on right now."

Joy looked away, embarrassed to say such things even if they were her true feelings. "I just thought things would be different when Faith was born. I thought I'd get some acknowledgement and wouldn't be ignored. Now, it's all about Mercy and Honor because now they're having their second babies. And you're excited about going up to see them, but what about me? I never get any attention or fuss made and neither does Faith. Hardly anyone visits us." Joy sniffed back tears.

"Why do you feel you need attention from us anyway?

You've got your own family now. Doesn't Isaac give you enough attention. Is that what the real problem is?"

"Of course he does. He gives me plenty of attention, and he's such a good husband and a good father." Joy breathed out heavily. "I guess I always felt invisible growing up with a bunch of sisters. I wasn't the cute younger one, and I wasn't the oldest and more capable. It's hard being in the middle. I tried to be as good as I could and do the right thing, but no one cared."

"And you did, Joy. You were a *wunderbaar* example for the other girls to follow." *Mamm* smiled.

"No one followed me at all. They just made fun of me and talked about me behind my back. To them, I was just someone to laugh at."

"That's because you can be a bit serious sometimes."

Joy sighed. "You're not making me feel any better if that's what you came over here to do."

"I came to see what was bothering you, and now I know that you have a problem with me and how I raised you just like all the others do."

"What others?"

"I didn't do the right thing by any of my *kinner*, according to them. Earl has got some ridiculous mindset against me, and I don't know what I did to him."

Joy sighed again. "This is my point. It's never about me, it's always about the others. You came here to talk to me about why I felt a certain way and when you get here, you talk about them. It's never about me. When will I get any of the attention that I deserve? I can't help being born in the middle."

"Hope doesn't complain, and she's also in the middle."

"She's busy with Fairfax. He keeps her occupied for the moment, but she has said some things to me, and she feels it too."

"You're basically upset because of the order of your birth?"

"I guess so. That's probably how it started."

"That's rubbish. What about me?" *Mamm* asked. "What would I do for a simple thank you from one of you saying I was a *gut mudder* and did a *wunderbaar* job? Do you know how hard it was raising six girls?"

Joy knew how hard it must've been, especially now that she had a baby of her own. But it annoyed her that Wilma was making excuses for everything when she was trying her best to explain her feelings. What was the point? "Did you come over here to complain, Mother?"

"No, I didn't. I'm sorry, I'm just upset with all of you. And you probably don't know the news yet."

Joy's eyebrows rose. "What news is that?"

"They brought the wedding forward."

"Ah, that. I found out from Christina a few days ago. I don't think we'll be able to go anyway. It'll be too hard with the baby, and besides that, someone needs to stay and work. I think—"

Mamm gritted her teeth. "And I suppose Christina found out from Mark."

"That's right."

"And I was the last to know. Do you see what I mean? It wears me down that everybody has a problem with how I raised you all. I was doing the best I possibly could. You all complain that I didn't give this one enough attention and I didn't give that one enough attention; it becomes a heavy burden after a while. How will you feel if Faith comes back to you unhappy with what you've done in twenty years time?"

"I'm going to give her all the attention I can. I'm hoping I don't have that problem. "

"Ah, but you might."

"I don't think you're taking this seriously, *Mamm*. All you've done since you've got here is complain about other people. Do you see what my problem is? Everybody overshadows me. I thought that would change when Faith was born. I thought I might get some attention, but people rarely visit me."

"You said that already and I heard you."

"Christina is the one who visits me the most."

"That's because she doesn't have a child of her own. She's always looking after Iris too. If she had her own child, you'd barely see her."

"That might be the case, but at least I have someone who's visiting me."

"I see. Thank you for telling me why you're upset. It's not the answer I thought I'd get, but I'll accept it. I will visit you more often and encourage the others to do so as well."

Joy was pleased her mother was finally allowing her words to sink in. "Thank you, that would be a start. And before you say it, it's hard for me to get over there since we only have the one buggy."

"I thought Mark picked up Isaac and took him to and from work."

"Only sometimes."

"I'll try to do better, Joy. It's hard to give every child

equal attention. I didn't know I'd have to do that for the rest of their lives, though."

"Only the ones who have been ignored. *Denke, Mamm."*

"Back on that other subject, what do you think about Earl and Miriam getting married so soon? They weren't meant to get married until the end of the year. It upsets me that they brought the date forward. What is going on?"

"They're in love, and they obviously couldn't wait to start their life together."

Mamm tapped a finger on her chin. "I can't help wondering if it was more than that."

"What are you thinking, *Mamm?"*

"I wonder if they're doing it to spite me?"

Joy laughed. "I doubt that it would've had anything to do with you. Why would you think it would?"

"I just worry that he didn't take my and Ada's advice. We told him about the age gap."

Her mother would do better to stay out of Earl's life, but she couldn't hurt her feelings by telling her that. "He obviously knew about the age gap and didn't care. I'm surprised you mentioned it to him. No wonder he left so upset."

Mamm looked down at her hands folded in her lap. "Ada and I thought we had to say some things. It was my duty as a mother to say what I thought of the pairing."

"Was that your idea or Ada's idea?"

She looked over at Joy and wiggled her nose. "It was both. I know you think Ada influences me, but she doesn't. We think the same about so many things, and that's why she's been my friend for so many years."

"I guess so."

Wilma rubbed her nose. "This place smells like dog."

"Oh, I'm sorry. I didn't know."

Mamm rose to her feet. "I'll have to go. I'll stay longer next time and hopefully, she'll be awake."

Joy got up to walk her out.

CHAPTER TWENTY-FIVE

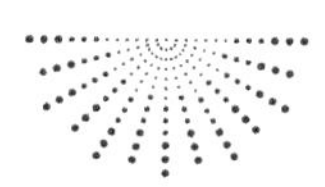

Cherish had a hard time waiting for Wilma to get back in the buggy. All this time alone had only caused her to worry again about the stories that might come out.

She had to warn *Mamm* about what was sure to happen. If Krystal were writing a book, it'd get published sooner or later, and now Daniel was racing to get his news stories finished so he could beat Krystal to it.

Nothing could stop them now. She'd done all she could.

When Wilma climbed up into the buggy an hour and a half later, Cherish said, "I just need to tell you something."

"Let's just get the buggy moving, Cherish. I have to go to the bathroom."

"You could've gone at Joy's."

"I didn't want to."

"Okay."

Mamm twisted to study Cherish. "What's so important so suddenly?"

"It's not good."

"I didn't think it would be. What have you done now?"

"Nothing." Cherish opened her mouth and let it all flow out. "Remember Daniel, the reporter?"

"Yes," *Mamm* said, cautiously.

"Firstly, Daniel is going to write about us and say that when we found out Krystal wasn't rich we told her to leave."

"That's not true at all. He can't write that."

"Yes, he can. Reporters don't always report the truth. He doesn't let the truth get in the way of a good story. That's what he told me once."

"It simply isn't true."

Cherish took her eyes off the road for a second to look at her mother. "I know, *Mamm,* that's the problem."

"We had that girl at our house for months and months."

"I know."

Mamm continued, "We were nothing but nice to her, took her everywhere, and treated her like one of the family."

"I know."

"And all along, she was deceiving us."

Cherish nodded. "And that's not all."

"What else will he say?"

"When Krystal was at the café a while back, and we were all sitting down with Daniel, she happened to mention about a baby being born out of wedlock and then that baby growing up and coming back and marrying his mother's stepdaughter."

"Well, that part's true."

"I know, but do you want that to get out?"

"Do you mean he knows it was me who had the child?" Wilma asked.

"Yes."

"That would be unfortunate if he wrote that." Deep worry lines appeared on *Mamm's* face.

"I know that's why I've been trying to stop him."

"Oh, dear." *Mamm* put her hand over her mouth.

"And now I find out he's been talking to Krystal, and she's going to write a book about the whole thing."

"You can't get a whole book out of that."

"A book about her stay with us, and who knows what lies she'll add in the book."

"No one will believe it, will they?" *Mamm's* bottom lip quivered.

"I think they will. That's why I'm so worried. Now Daniel knows she's writing it, he's trying to be first with the story. Except someone attacked him, and he's in the hospital for a few more days."

"I see. You can't do much from a hospital bed, can you?"

"It's what he'll do when he gets out that I'm worried about."

"I won't worry about it at all. People can think what they like, say what they like. There's nothing we can do about it."

"But, *Mamm...*"

"I can't care about anyone finding out anymore. All I

can think about right now is being there at the birth of my two new grandchildren. That's what's important. I don't have the energy to be upset about someone saying what happened a long time ago."

"I thought you'd be upset."

"It happened, and I'm not proud of it. I made mistakes, but I'm not the only one who's done that."

Cherish had to ask the question. "Does the bishop know?"

"Yes. What I did back then was the best thing for Carter. And as you know, my sister, Iris, eventually married Carter's father. He had his father there when he was growing up. Two loving parents raised him."

"And you didn't find that out for a long time later."

"That's right. So, he was raised by his birth father and his aunt and that's not a bad start in life, don't you think?" Wilma asked.

"Yes, it turned out well for him. He's such a nice person." Cherish recalled that Carter never found out until later that Iris wasn't his real mother, that she was his aunt.

"I think we can both agree on that, Cherish. So don't worry yourself over my feelings."

"But you're always saying things about bringing shame to the family—don't you think that will be enough to do it?"

"Most likely."

"Oh, I thought you'd care more. And he's also going to say that we only got rid of Krystal when we found out she wasn't Caroline, and we learned we were looking after a girl with no money."

"He can say what he likes, Cherish, but no one is going to believe a silly story in the newspaper."

"It kind of sounds a bit believable to me as well as being shocking."

"Then you should stop believing everything you hear and start thinking." *Mamm* tapped the side of her head. "Use your brain."

"Okay, I'll use my brain. That's a big relief now that you don't care. I tried to stop them."

"I'm not worried."

Cherish couldn't work out why her mother was being so calm about it. It seemed a little odd. She never could understand her mother.

"My girls have moved away to have their babies elsewhere. Florence only talks to me because she has to, and Joy is upset with me for no good reason. So if someone wants to tell lies, I can't stop them."

Cherish didn't want to upset her mother by saying that not all of it would be lies. "Okay, if you don't care neither do I. I guess one of us should tell Levi about this."

"I will tell him."

"Denke, Mamm." Cherish was relieved about that. It was one less thing she'd have to do.

"Oh, and Cherish."

"Jah?"

"Visit Joy more often, would you?"

"Sure."

LATER THAT NIGHT, Cherish was with the other girls peeling the vegetables when Levi came into the room.

"Cherish, I think you and I need to have a little talk."

She stood up. "Here, or where?"

"In the living room."

Once they were seated, he began, although she already guessed what it was about.

"Your mother told me you're worried about the reporter."

"I was, but *Mamm's* not worried so neither am I." She leaned forward. "Are you worried?"

Levi said, "No. Wilma is right. We can't worry about what others will do or say, Cherish. As long as we can lay our heads on our pillows knowing we have done right that day, that's all we can do. Unless you want the bishop to have a talk with him."

"Nee. That wouldn't do any good. Thanks anyway. I don't think that will do any good."

"I don't want you to worry. It's useless getting upset about things we can't change."

Cherish nodded, but she couldn't help feeling she could've done more. Tomorrow, she'd go to the hospital and make one last effort with Daniel. She'd have to do it late in the day after her chores. This time, she'd make Daniel see sense. "May I take out a horse and buggy tomorrow after I finish my work?"

"Do you want to visit your friends?"

"Yes." She didn't want to let Levi know she was going back there or he'd be suspicious.

"Okay. That should be fine."

"Denke, Levi. Do you want me to bring you anything?"

"I'm fine. I'll just sit here and wait until someone calls me for dinner."

Cherish headed back to cut the vegetables with the others. Tomorrow, she'd have to do what she did today—leave the buggy at a friend's house and then get a taxi to the hospital.

CHAPTER TWENTY-SIX

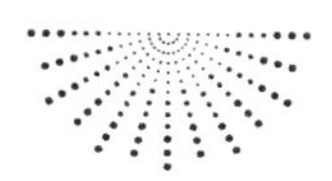

Cherish walked into Daniel's hospital room, where she'd been the day before. To her surprise, both Daniel and the bed were gone.

A man in a dark gray suit sat in the corner of the room, staring at her. Cherish noticed his suit was expensive and his black shoes were made from high-quality soft leather. He looked like a man of importance. A *handsome* man of importance.

"Where is Daniel?" she asked.

"Taking x-rays. He'll be back in a minute."

"Oh, good."

"And you are…?"

"A friend of his, come to see how he's doing. Are you a relative?"

"No, I'm his lawyer. That is, I hope to be."

Cherish moved closer. "What does he need a lawyer for?"

"Seems he had an accident, and he might have cause to sue someone."

"I heard he didn't know who attacked him."

"Is that right?"

"I think so unless something has changed. He probably doesn't know the truth from a lie. Oh, I shouldn't say that. It's just that he doesn't care about what he writes."

"That is disappointing. And how do you know him?"

"He did a story on my family once. The story was about my father... my stepfather, I should say, and my family's apple orchard."

"The Baker Apple Orchard?"

"Yes. You know it?" she asked, feeling a little more at ease.

"I do. I've bought apples there and pickles and so on. Why have you come to see him?"

"I told you already."

"My truth meter tells me there's something you're holding back. You're not here just to see how he is, are you?"

Cherish leaned against the wall. "No. I was here yesterday too. I asked him to stop writing the stories he intends to write about my family."

"Oh?" He looked at her in such a way that she felt compelled to say more.

"It's all lies, well, except for some of it."

The man jumped up and handed Cherish his card. "Name's Travis Johnson, attorney at law. If you're serious about stopping him and he's refusing, you might need the strength of the law behind you."

She took the card from him and looked down at the gold lettering on the glossy white card. "Sounds impressive, but I'm not sure what that all means."

"There are various legal means you have at your disposal. You can stop him with an injunction against him or his newspaper, or both."

"I didn't know that." She was pleased she'd come for a final talk with Daniel. "And how do I go about doing that?"

"You can retain my services."

Once again, she looked at his suit, crisp white shirt, and blue and white silk tie. "Sounds kind of expensive."

"It needn't be."

"That's not the only problem I've got."

He grabbed a chair from the other side of the room and placed it close to him. "Sit."

She sat in front of him.

"Details!" he demanded.

"It's a long story."

"I don't need all the details yet. Give me an outline."

"Well, we had a girl staying with us, and she lied about who she was." She told him the whole story about Caroline and how Krystal had been impersonating her, and about Krystal threatening to write a book. "So, you see, Daniel's idea was to say that, as soon as we found out she wasn't the rich girl, Caroline, we told her to go. And that's totally untrue because my stepfather asked her to go before we discovered she wasn't rich. She also lied about her house burning down when it never did."

"I can see that would be distressing. No matter. Have you got this girl's address?"

"Sure have."

"We can send her an injunction too."

"Okay." Cherish was liking this law stuff very much if

it stopped people from doing horrible things. "What does it take to be a lawyer?"

"Lots of long years of study."

"That's no good. I'll cross that off my career list."

He burst out laughing, then stopped and looked into her eyes. "Under the circumstances, I don't know if you should be talking to him at all. I mean, what's the point?"

"You're probably right. I have asked him to stop what he's doing. I just wanted one last try. But, just a minute, can you be my lawyer and his lawyer at the same time?"

His eyebrows drew together. "No. Have you retained my services yet?"

"How much does it cost?"

"Depends on how much work needs to be done. I can write the initial letter. There's a good chance that will work. It'll be close to one hundred dollars per letter, so that makes two hundred dollars."

Cherish sighed inwardly. Why was everything troublesome in her life coming out at two hundred dollars? "I don't know if a letter will do it. I think I might prefer the conjunction."

"The injunction. That can be a more selective process."

"And the cost?"

An orderly wheeled Daniel and his bed back into the room.

Daniel looked at Travis. "Are you still hangin' around here? I told you I don't need a lawyer. If I do, I'll call you. I've got your card." Then he looked at Cherish. "What are *you* doing back here?"

Cherish sprang to her feet. "Don't worry. I'm not staying."

"Cherish, I want to—" Daniel was interrupted by the lawyer.

"That's enough." Travis stood up and grabbed Cherish's arm. "Don't say anything to him. Let's go." He moved Cherish out of the room.

"Why couldn't I talk to him?" she asked when they were well away from his room. He let her arm go. He was so close she could smell his aftershave.

"It might compromise the situation."

They walked to the elevator, and he pressed the button.

"Can I meet you at your office tomorrow to talk about this further?" She wondered where she'd get the two hundred from when she still needed to find the money for the barn. Two hundred for the barn and two hundred for the lawyer was four hundred. She wasn't that good at math, but she was better when it had a dollar sign in front.

"Why don't I meet you at a café? In the meantime, I'll look into what I can do for you."

"Perfect. Thank you."

"We can meet at the café next door to the library. Do you know the one?"

"I do." The elevator arrived, and they got in and then the door closed.

"I'll see when I've got a time slot available." He pulled out his phone and clicked a couple of times. "I've got a spot free at two o'clock."

"Four is better for me, or even half-past three."

He looked back at his phone. "I could switch some things around and meet you at half-past three."

The doors opened.

"Perfect, I'll see you then." Cherish headed out to catch a taxi.

That meant she could work in the orchard up until two and then hopefully slip away unnoticed and get into town just after three.

She got a taxi back to her friend's place where her horse and buggy were being minded. Then Cherish headed home.

CHAPTER TWENTY-SEVEN

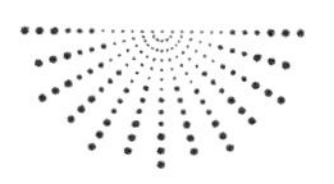

The next day, Cherish had nearly finished her assigned work by 2 o'clock. Surely Florence wouldn't notice if she snuck off a bit early.

As she walked away, she heard, "Cherish, where are you going?"

Cherish's heart sank into her lace-up boots. She'd only walked two steps in the direction of the house. She turned around to face Florence. "I have a meeting in town."

Florence folded her arms. "This is the first time I've heard anything about it. Who is the meeting with?"

"A lawyer."

"A *lawyer*? A lawyer about what?"

"Krystal is going to write a book about our family and tell a lot of lies. The reporter who wrote about the orchard is writing the same as Krystal. He's also going to write about how Carter came to be here at the farm, and about *Mamm.*"

"Why didn't you come to me about this?"

"I didn't think of it."

"You should've if it involves Carter. Who is this reporter?"

"Daniel Whitcombe."

"Ah, yes. I vaguely remember him. You should stay away from people like that."

"He's in the hospital. That's where I met this lawyer. He said he could do something illegal to stop him from telling the story."

Florence frowned. "You mean something legal?"

"I don't know the word."

"For a start, I don't know if there's anything he can do. Lawyers are expensive. I think you can only do something after he writes the story. I'm not too sure about it."

"He sounded like he knew what he was talking about. He does look a little young to be a lawyer, now that I think about it. He doesn't have gray hair or anything."

Florence sighed. "Exactly how much are you paying this lawyer?"

"Nothing yet. That's why I'm going to meet him today. He's going to tell me how much it would cost."

"Do Wilma or Levi know anything about this?"

"No. They say they aren't worried, but I know they are. Who wouldn't be? You know how *Mamm* is always worried about shame coming upon the family. And this would bring terrible shame, and all her secrets would be exposed. I don't think many people know about it."

"Carter has friends that are lawyers. You should've come to me. Come over to the house and tell him what's going on."

"I can't right now."

"You can. Come with me now."

"But I've got a meeting scheduled. I can't say I'll meet him somewhere and not turn up."

"I guess you can't. Meet with this lawyer and see what he has to say, but don't agree to anything. Don't pay any money, and certainly don't sign anything."

"Don't sign anything, don't pay anything, and don't agree to anything. Got it."

"That's right. Remember that, Cherish, because this is very serious, and you don't want to get yourself into trouble."

"I'm trying to keep myself out of trouble and the rest of the family too."

"Thank you, Cherish, that is good of you, but you should've come to Carter."

"I honestly didn't think of it. I best hitch the buggy now or I'll be late."

"Why don't you have Carter drive you there?"

"No, Florence, I hate to bother him, and the lawyer is not expecting two of us. He's only expecting me."

Florence narrowed her eyes. "I'm not so sure I should be allowing you to go, but you should be fine if you just remember everything I said."

"I will."

Cherish hitched the buggy as quickly as she could. When she was driving away from the house, she remembered that as a young girl, she could never get anything by Florence. She'd forgotten how strict life was before Florence left to marry Carter.

Cherish arrived at the café at 3:35, so the clock on the wall told her. She'd thought she'd be late because of the discussion with Florence, but Travis was nowhere to be seen.

She sat down in a booth and waited, reviewing what Florence had told her: No agreements; no signatures; no money. Just when she was nearly losing all hope that he'd show, the door swung open. Travis hurried toward her, smoothing down his hair. Smiling at her, he then sat down in front of her, placing his briefcase at the end of the table.

It wasn't acceptable to keep her waiting. "I was beginning to think you weren't coming."

"Sorry I'm so late. I've had one of those days." He passed her one of the menus on the table and took one for himself. "What are you having?"

"Nothing." She put the menu to one side.

"You have to have something. You can't just sit here and have nothing."

"Coffee, then."

He snapped his fingers to get the attention of the waitress. Cherish involuntarily cringed, glad to note Travis hadn't seen her reaction. She was a waitress, and she hated it when people snapped their fingers like that at her, and so did all the people she worked with.

The waitress walked over.

"Two coffees, please."

"Anything else?"

He shook his head. "No thanks."

When the waitress left, Cherish couldn't wait any longer. "Last time we talked, you were going to look into things."

"I have, and it's not going to be as easy as I first

thought. Do you know for certain that these two individuals intend to publish your stories?"

"They've said so."

"It would be an invasion of privacy and possibly libel, depending on what they say. It's not a crime as such, but it is a civil matter, and you can sue for damages. It's a little more difficult to stop them before they've started."

"What does all that mean exactly?"

"Normally, this kind of thing is done after the stories are published."

"Well, that wouldn't be much good because once the stories are published, they're out there."

"That's true."

Cherish put her elbows on the table and plopped her chin into her hands. "I was hoping this was the answer."

"At this stage, the best course of action is to appeal to their sense of fairness. Let me write a letter to each, telling them how it will affect you and your family."

"I don't know. Can I think about it for a while?" She was concerned about the money and where she was going to get it.

"Sure, but if you're worried, I wouldn't leave it too long."

"I'll have to talk it over with my family first."

"Okay. Can't argue with that."

The waitress brought the coffees.

He took a sip and then said, "What do you do? Do you work other than in your family's famous apple orchard?"

"I work in a café." She told him which one it was.

"I've never gone there, but I have gone to your family's

shop at the apple orchard. It would be good if it were open year round."

It wouldn't be good for me, Cherish thought, since she liked to do as little work as possible. "You should come to the cafe sometime. I'm mostly there on a Tuesday."

He smiled. "Maybe I will."

Cherish wrapped her hands around the coffee mug. She was too nervous to drink it, but she forced herself to take a sip since he'd have to pay for it.

"Would you like something to eat?"

"No, I'll be fine. You have something if you want. Don't you have to get back to work?"

"Yeah. I won't eat. I'm used to working through and not getting anything to eat until I go home."

She laughed. "I guess you do. So is this your lunch break? It's rather late."

"I guess you could call it that. I'd like to help you out, Cherish Baker."

"Thank you."

"I hate talking about money, but if that's a problem for you..."

"It is a bit because I have to find the money for a barn repair."

He frowned at her.

Cherish giggled. "Don't ask. It's a long story."

He smiled. "I'd like to hear it sometime. I could take my fee in apples."

"That would be an awful lot of apples."

"Apple products. Pies, apple sauce, whatever. Works out for you, works out for me."

"Thank you. I'll mention that to my stepfather when I tell him that you can write letters for us."

He took another mouthful of coffee. "It's not just that I'm writing a letter. If people get a letter from a lawyer, they know their client is serious. They won't want to mess around and get involved in a legal battle."

"And I'd be the client?"

"Yes."

Cherish sighed. "My mother said she doesn't mind if the story comes out, but I know she does. It's just her being brave."

"I hope for your sake the story doesn't come out."

"Yeah, me too. It would be awful." The stress of everything made her eyes sting, and she knew tears were forming. She blinked a couple of times to keep them away. One tear trickled down her cheek, and she hoped he wouldn't notice.

He stared at her, and his eyebrows rose as he leaned over and wiped away her tear.

Warmth flooded through Cherish. There was something different about this man. He was so caring, and his touch was so sensitive and soft.

He smiled. "Was it something I said?"

She shook her head. "No, I'm just thinking about things too much, hoping my family doesn't suffer."

"Don't say another word. I know what it's like coming from a small town, and I'm guessing your community would be the same. Everyone knows everyone else's business or they think they do. If the story comes out, it'll be the talk of the town for months or even years."

"People are so judgmental sometimes."

"It's true. Everyone judges even if they say they don't."

Cherish's lips turned down at the corners. "So you're saying all this to make me feel better? Because it's not working."

He laughed. "Sorry, my mouth has a habit of running away with me. I'm trying to get that under control."

"Yeah, I know how that can be. I have that same problem."

He drained his coffee. "How old are you, Cherish?"

"How old do I look?"

He laughed again while wagging a finger at her. "Don't play that game. It's too hard to say."

"Go on, guess."

"I'm hopeless at guessing ages. I'd say anything between fifteen and twenty-five."

"You're right."

"You're not going to tell me?"

She wondered why he wanted to know. "Oh, do I have to be over eighteen to hire you?"

He rubbed his neck. "That's a good question. I'll look into it."

"You're new to all this, aren't you?"

"How can you tell?"

"Because you have to look into everything."

"Not everything." He made a face and then pulled his cell phone out of his inner coat pocket. "Just a minute." He pressed a couple of buttons, read something, and then looked back at her. "You can hire a lawyer even if you're under eighteen." He smiled as he set the phone down on the table. "I guess you've answered my question about how old you are."

"Not really."

"You're under eighteen."

"Yes," she admitted.

He laughed.

"It's not funny."

"I'm sorry. I know it's not. It is a bit funny that you wouldn't tell me."

Cherish was a little surprised that he was so easy to talk with. It was just like talking to one of her friends. "It's just that people make a big deal out of ages. I think as soon as people are adults, age should not come into it. It shouldn't even be talked about."

"Hmm. Then there'd be no birthdays. No birthday cake. I'm partial to cake."

"Well, people could still celebrate their birthdays and not make a big deal about what age they are."

He smiled at her. Then glanced at his wristwatch. "Ah, I've got to go. I'm sorry. I'll see you soon?"

She nodded.

He stood up, pulled out a twenty-dollar bill, left it on the table, grabbed his briefcase, and then hurried out the door.

CHAPTER TWENTY-EIGHT

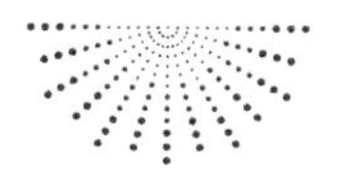

It was two weeks later, and Cherish was working in a section of the orchard close to the house. When she heard a car coming up the drive, she stood on her tiptoes. She saw someone who looked like Daniel Whitcombe get out of the vehicle.

She dropped what she was doing and went closer.

Florence saw her. "Get back here, Cherish. What are you doing? I gave you a job to do; now do it."

"It's the reporter."

"It's probably just someone asking when the shop will be open. Tell them it'll be open in the summer months."

"It's Daniel. I can see him." Ignoring Florence, she hurried to see why Daniel was there. It couldn't have been for anything pleasant.

Daniel was walking with one crutch, and he had his hand on the porch railing just about to walk up the porch steps when she called out to him.

He looked around, and she slowly walked toward him. His face didn't give away a thing. Would he have come where he knew he wasn't welcome? Unless... unless he'd changed his mind.

"Daniel, how are you?"

"Better, thanks. I'm doing fine." He nodded at the crutch. "I won't need this for much longer. Only a week or so."

"Oh, good."

"I got a letter from your lawyer."

Cherish couldn't believe it. She hadn't instructed Travis to write anything, not yet. She gulped. "You did?"

Leaning on the crutch, he looked down at the ground. "I got carried away with this whole journalism thing, thought I was going to be the next TV presenter on 60 Minutes or something."

"You don't want that anymore?"

He looked at her as he inched forward. "I've come to realize that when there are so many obstacles put in someone's way, maybe they're not obstacles, maybe they're warning signs." His face softened. "Could be I was on the wrong path."

She recalled their conversation at the hospital. He'd yelled at her to stop talking about paths. "You think that?"

"Someone told me that once. Not in so many words, but that was the gist of it."

Relief washed over Cherish. Even though he hadn't said it outright yet, it seemed he was changing his mind.

"Maybe there's another career out there for me. And you know what?"

"What?" She held her breath.

"I randomly got a call from a big New York City realtor. He wants me on his team."

"He does?"

"Yes." He looked up at the sky. "I've always wanted to give real estate a go."

Cherish couldn't believe her ears, and she sent up a quick prayer of thanks. "How did the realtor know about you?"

"He heard about me somehow. Heard I was a go-getter."

"So you're not going to be a reporter anymore?" She had to know for certain.

"No." He looked in her eyes. "Your stories are safe, Cherish. I'm sorry to have put you through what I did. I know it was horrible, but in the end, when nothing was working for me, I got impatient and didn't see any other way of getting ahead. It isn't very nice when I look back on it now. I think I can be an ethical realtor."

"That sounds great. I'm so happy for you."

He nodded. "I've got a cousin in New York. We grew up like brothers. His friend, who was living in his apartment has just moved out so I'm moving in."

"That sounds perfect. So you've already been hired for the job?"

"I have. I'll start in leasing and rentals, then work my way up to sales—penthouses or maybe development projects. Some of those apartments go for millions, you know."

"Do they?"

"Yes. I can make a ton of money, more than if I stayed here doing what I was doing."

"I hope everything goes well for you. When do you have to be there?"

"Tomorrow. No point in wasting time."

"There's not." Cherish was in shock, then he started walking away. He was almost to his car, so she caught up with him. "Wait."

He turned around and looked at her.

"You said you were in touch with Krystal?"

"I have talked to her recently. She's the one who contacts me. Why do you ask?"

Cherish licked her lips. "Is there any chance she's going to write something? She told Favor she's writing a book."

He laughed. "I wouldn't worry about her. She's got other things on her mind."

Cherish put her hand on her chest. "I'm so glad to hear that."

He opened his car door.

Cherish stepped closer. "Thank you, Daniel. You've got no idea how relieved I am."

"Again, I'm sorry I was a jerk."

"Will I ever see you again?"

"Maybe. I'll be back here some time to visit my family."

Cherish couldn't help liking him even though he had given her some rough moments. "Please stop by and say hello when you're back."

"Do you want me to, after everything I've done to upset you?" He leaned on the crutch.

She inhaled deeply. She wasn't one to hold a grudge. "Everyone makes mistakes."

"No hard feelings?" He put his hand out, and she shook it.

"Not a one."

He smiled at her, and then he carefully put his crutch in first before he slid into the driver's seat.

Cherish stepped back and watched him turn the car around and then drive away.

CHAPTER TWENTY-NINE

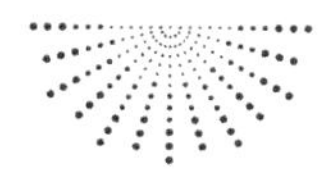

Florence walked up to Cherish. "Was that the reporter?"

"Yes, and he's dropped the stories. He's not going to write them anymore."

"That's good. Now you've got nothing to worry about."

She didn't want to mention Krystal. Daniel thought their former guest wouldn't be a problem. Cherish wasn't so sure. "He's going to New York to be a realtor."

"That's a surprise. Well, you officially got out of the last fifteen minutes of work."

"I'm sorry, Florence. I'll make up for it."

Florence hugged her. "Are you okay?"

"I am now."

"I'll see you tomorrow, Cherish."

"Yes, and I'll work half an hour extra, I promise I will."

When Florence walked away, she realized that Carter must've got Daniel his dream job. Florence must've told him all about it. Carter was wealthy, and he knew all kinds of rich people. They were all his friends. She'd have to thank him, but there was one thing she had to do first. She had to call Malachi and tell him the good news. She'd call Ruth and leave a message for Malachi to call her back.

She hurried to the barn and picked up the address book, and thumbed through it, looking for Ruth's phone number. As she was doing that, the phone rang.

She picked up the receiver. "Hello?"

"Cherish?"

"Yes. Is that you, Malachi?"

"It is."

"I was just looking for Ruth's number so I could get a message to you to call me."

"That's amazing. Now you don't have to."

"Don't have to do what?"

"Call Ruth."

She closed the book. "No, I don't." Then she realized he probably had terrible news. "What is it?"

"I've got somethin' great to tell you."

"What?"

"A neighbor was pulling down a barn, and I was able to retrieve his whole back wall. The wood is excellent. It's like new. We can use some of that, we can use most of that wood to repair the barn, and it won't cost us one cent."

She was so relieved she didn't have to think about the money. Not the money for the lawyer, and now, not the money for the barn. God had answered her prayers. She sent up a quick thank you. "Thank you so much, Malachi. Today is the day of good news."

He laughed. "What else has happened?"

"It seems Daniel Whitcombe is going to be a realtor. He got an offer from someone he didn't know. He's leaving to go to his new job, and he won't write the stories."

"That's great news. I'm so pleased for you, Cherish. Everything is working out for you."

"Thanks. I know."

"He'll be far away in New York, too. He'll never have to bother you again."

Cherish frowned. She'd never mentioned where Daniel was going. "Wait. Did you have anything to do with him going?"

There was a long hesitation. "Why would you ask that?"

"I never mentioned he was going to New York, so how would you have known unless..."

There was silence on the other end of the phone.

"Malachi, you need to tell me what's going on and you need to tell me now."

He grunted. "Me and my big mouth. Okay, I'll admit I happen to know a guy who insisted he owed me a favor. Now he doesn't."

"Who is that?"

"Just some guy who owns some big real estate business."

"You had him contact Daniel and offer him a job?"

"That's right. I'm sure Daniel will do well. From what you said, he's pretty driven for success."

Cherish couldn't believe it. "He is. How can I ever repay you, Malachi? You saved me money for the barn, and you got Daniel out of doing that story, and he'll probably enjoy real estate better. He was stuck in a job where he couldn't get ahead."

"Great."

Great? Is that all he had to say? "Malachi, I asked you and you said you were only praying."

"I know, but you know what the Bible says about prayer? You have to add works because without works, faith is—"

Cherish interrupted, "Dead. I do recall that. Out of interest, just what did you do for this New York guy for him to do you such a favor?"

"Ah, Cherish, I can't give away all my secrets, can I?"

"Yes, you can. I won't tell anybody. You've got to tell me." She held her breath, hoping he'd tell her. Malachi could be so stubborn sometimes.

He was silent for a while. "It's a long story and one best left until I see you again."

"I can't wait that long, Malachi." She was so thankful to him. She had to do something nice for him.

"Ah, I think you can wait, Cherish. Anyway, I need to have something to make you come back, sooner other than later."

Now she was intrigued. How would Malachi know a man like that? "Don't do that to me. It could be a long time before I return and I hate not knowing things. I hope to get there at the end of the year, but who knows?"

He laughed. "You'll be incredibly bored once you hear the story. I've got to go. I'm at Ruth's usin' her phone, and she's glarin' at me."

"I am not," Cherish heard Ruth say.

"Say hello to her for me, and I'll talk to you later. Thank you so, so much. I owe you a good deed or even two." She hung up the phone's receiver. She still felt so bad that she had thought Malachi had anything to do with Daniel's attack. Nothing made sense. What did make sense was her family's stories were safe, and that was all that mattered.

Cherish walked out of the barn to the sounds of laughter. She turned to the noise and saw Bliss and Adam playing with Cottonball in the outdoor rabbit enclosure. Caramel sat on the other side, looking on with his head tilted curiously.

Hearing a buggy, she turned to the left and saw it was Fairfax arriving for Hope.

Then Cherish spotted Favor and *Mamm* sitting on the porch eating cake. Joy and baby Faith were with them.

Cherish couldn't keep the smile from her face. Life was pretty close to perfect.

Her family's secrets were safe; both Daniel and Krystal were gone. Her barn was being repaired at no cost, and she no longer had to worry about finding money for anything.

She looked around herself and took a deep breath.

It was Spring; the sun was warm on her skin, and life was wonderful, for now...

There was just one more call Cherish had to make.

She walked back into the dark barn and lifted the phone's receiver. When he answered, she said. "You sent a letter to the reporter?"

"Cherish Baker?"

"Yes."

"I sent out two letters to the people you were worried about."

"I didn't tell you to, but it worked out perfectly. Daniel is getting out of writing for the paper, and he said Krystal won't publish the book. He was unclear why he thought that. How much do I owe you?"

"Nothing."

Cherish didn't know if she'd heard correctly. "You told me about a hundred dollars each letter."

"I didn't have any other work on my plate, and I felt like doing something good. Chalk it up to pro bono."

"I don't know what that means. You did the work; you must be paid."

"Ah, that is a technical point of law. Do I deserve to be paid if you didn't officially give me the job?"

"I think so."

"Not according to the law. That's what 'pro bono' means. Doing something good, not for the money but just because."

Cherish laughed. "I wouldn't know about anything like that. Let me pay you. I have to."

"How about you buy me a cup of coffee next time we bump into each other?"

Cherish said, "I'm so grateful, and you deserve to be paid. There's no likelihood we'll bump into each other."

"How about I meet you at that same coffee shop at two on Monday afternoon?"

"Ahh, I'm not sure." Cherish felt bad. He had saved her family a lot of heartaches. This man was a nice *Englisher,* but so was Daniel once too. Did she want to risk involvement with another man who pretended to be friendly only to show his true colors when she got to know him? She wasn't ready for another disappointment. Then she recalled how it felt when Travis had tenderly wiped that tear from her cheek. "Okay. I'll meet you at two on Monday. Do you like apple pies?"

"I love them. I'm sure I told you that."

"Just making sure. I'm going to make you a basket of food and you must take it."

He laughed. "I will, gladly. I'm a starving bachelor."

Cherish figured he was only being nice because he felt sorry for her. He was a man with everything going for him, so why would he want to be involved with a far-too-young Amish girl? She was kidding herself, but a girl could dream, couldn't she? "Thank you again, Travis, for all you've done. You've helped change my life."

"It was my pleasure."

"I'll see you Monday." She hung up the phone, wondering how she'd get off work early again on Monday. Hopefully, Florence would understand. Sometimes life was too busy to fit work in. Cherish wanted nothing more than to sit on the porch and join her mother and her sisters.

Before she got to the house, she noticed a car had turned off the road into the driveway. She stopped still and stared. Cherish had no idea who'd be visiting. Debbie wasn't arriving until tomorrow, so it was unlikely to be her.

Cherish sprinted to the house. "Who's in the car?" she asked no one in particular.

Bliss stood up and squinted at the vehicle. Then she gasped. "It's Debbie."

"Good thing we got her room ready today. I was told she was arriving tomorrow." Wilma pursed her lips disapprovingly.

"Let's go and help her carry her things." Cherish didn't want to be the only one or the first one to meet her.

The car stopped, and Debbie got out. She was a pleasant-looking girl with chubby cheeks. She looked similar to Bliss except for Debbie's dark hair. Bliss walked forward and hugged her.

It was then that Cherish noticed there was someone else in the car besides the driver.

The other car door opened, and...

Cherish's mouth dropped open, and it was as though the world stopped.

It was Krystal.

What was Krystal doing back here?

And why was she in the car with Debbie?

Thank you for reading Her Amish Farm.

www.SamanthaPriceAuthor.com

THE NEXT BOOK IN THE SERIES

Book 19

The Unsuitable Amish Wedding

Two unwanted guests, a road trip, and an Amish wedding!

Shortly after the family has said goodbye to one unwanted houseguest, Bliss's cousin arrives for an extended stay.
Cherish wants Debbie to fit in well with the family, but she's not too hopeful given some early warning signs.
Levi is left behind when Ada, Wilma, and the girls take a road trip to Ohio for Earl and Miriam's wedding.
Is it possible the pair will have a peaceful wedding without any outside interference?
Will Earl and Miriam get their happily ever after?

THE AMISH BONNET SISTERS

Book 1 Amish Mercy

Book 2 Amish Honor

Book 3 A Simple Kiss

Book 4 Amish Joy

Book 5 Amish Family Secrets

Book 6 The Englisher

Book 7 Missing Florence

Book 8 Their Amish Stepfather

Book 9 A Baby For Florence.

Book 10 Amish Bliss

Book 11 Amish Apple Harvest

Book 12 Amish Mayhem

Book 13 The Cost of Lies

Book 14 Amish Winter of Hope

Book 15 A Baby for Joy

Book 16 The Amish Meddler

Book 17 The Unsuitable Amish Bride

Book 18 Her Amish Farm

Book 19 The Unsuitable Amish Wedding

Book 20 Her Amish Secret

Book 21 Amish Harvest Mayhem

Book 22 Amish Family Quilt

Book 23 Hope's Amish Wedding

Book 24 A Heart of Hope

Book 25 A Season for Change

Book 26 Amish Farm Mayhem

Book 27 The Stolen Amish Wedding

Book 28 A Season for Second Chances

Book 29 A Change of Heart

Book 30 The Last Wedding

ALL SAMANTHA PRICE'S SERIES

Amish Maids Trilogy
A 3 book Amish romance series of novels featuring 5 friends finding love.

Amish Love Blooms
A 6 book Amish romance series of novels about four sisters and their cousins.

Amish Misfits
A series of 7 stand-alone books about people who have never fitted in.

The Amish Bonnet Sisters
To date there are 28 books in this continuing family saga. My most popular and best-selling series.

Amish Women of Pleasant Valley
An 8 book Amish romance series with the same characters. This has been one of my most popular series.

Ettie Smith Amish Mysteries
An ongoing cozy mystery series with octogenarian sleuths. Popular with lovers of mysteries such as Miss Marple or Murder She Wrote.

Amish Secret Widows' Society
A ten novella mystery/romance series - a prequel to the Ettie Smith Amish Mysteries.

Expectant Amish Widows
A stand-alone Amish romance series of 19 books.

Seven Amish Bachelors
A 7 book Amish Romance series following the Fuller brothers' journey to finding love.

Amish Foster Girls
A 4 book Amish romance series with the same characters who have been fostered to an Amish family.

Amish Brides
An Amish historical romance. 5 book series with the same characters who have arrived in America to start their new life.

Amish Romance Secrets
The first series I ever wrote. 6 novellas following the same characters.

Amish Christmas Books

Each year I write an Amish Christmas stand-alone romance novel.

Amish Twin Hearts
A 4 book Amish Romance featuring twins and their friends.

Amish Wedding Season
The second series I wrote. It has the same characters throughout the 5 books.

Amish Baby Collection
Sweet Amish Romance series of 6 stand-alone novellas.

Gretel Koch Jewel Thief
A clean 5 book suspense/mystery series about a jewel thief who has agreed to consult with the FBI.

Made in the USA
Monee, IL
04 October 2022